W9-AFJ-663

Four Souls

ALSO BY LOUISE ERDRICH

NOVELS
Love Medicine
The Beet Queen
Tracks
The Bingo Palace
Tales of Burning Love
The Antelope Wife
The Last Report on the Miracles at Little No Horse
The Master Butchers Singing Club

WITH MICHAEL DORRIS
The Crown of Columbus

POETRY
Jacklight
Baptism of Desire
Original Fire

FOR CHILDREN
Grandmother's Pigeon
The Birchbark House
The Range Eternal

NONFICTION
The Blue Jay's Dance
Books and Islands in Ojibwe Country

Four Souls

Louise Erdrich

HarperCollins*Publishers*

FOUR SOULS. Copyright © 2004 by Louise Erdrich. All rights reserved. Printed in the United States of America. No part of this book may be used or reproduced in any manner whatsoever without written permission except in the case of brief quotations embodied in critical articles and reviews. For information, address HarperCollins Publishers Inc., 10 East 53rd Street, New York, NY 10022.

HarperCollins books may be purchased for educational, business, or sales promotional use. For information, please write: Special Markets Department, HarperCollins Publishers Inc., 10 East 53rd Street, New York, NY 10022.

Grateful acknowledgment is made to the editors of *The New Yorker,* where portions of chapters 9 and 11 first appeared in slightly different form as "Love Snares."

Nothing in this book is true of anyone alive or dead.

FIRST EDITION

Designed by Elliott Beard

Family tree hand-lettered by Martie Holmer

Library of Congress Cataloging-in-Publication Data
Erdrich, Louise.
    Four souls : a novel / Louise Erdrich.—1st ed.
        p.   cm.
    ISBN 0-06-620975-7
    1. Indian women—Crimes against—Fiction. 2. Identity (Psychology)—Fiction. 3. Minneapolis (Minn.)—Fiction. 4. Ojibwa Indians—Fiction. 5. Indian women—Fiction. 6. North Dakota—Fiction. 7. Laundresses—Fiction. 8. Land tenure—Fiction. 9. Rich people—Fiction. 10. Revenge—Fiction. I. Title.
    PS3555.R42F   2004
    813'.54—dc22   2003065243

04 05 06 07 08   10 9 8 7 6 5 4 3 2 1

She threw out one soul and it came back hungry.

Kaanish inaa indinaawemaaganitog,

Asemaa ingii pagichige chi otaapin aawat atasookanag.
Aya ii onji wegonen ina pichi tazhimag kaaye
pichi ozhibii'wag kaagi aaya sig.

Kaawiin wiin aawiya nibaapinenimaasi.
Pepekaan inenimishig.

Miigwech,

Weweni sago.

Mirage Under the Ground

Margaret ==== Nanapush Anaquot (Four Demeter
Kashpaw   Souls; Ogimaakwe) Hawes
(Rushes Bear)   Gheen

      Fleur =·=·= (2) John (1) =·=·= Placide Polly
      Pillager   James Gheen Elizabeth
           Mauser   Gheen

Eli   Lulu
Kashpaw Nanapush

  Nestor   John James
  Kashpaw Mauser II

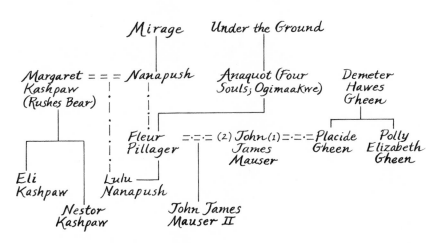

LEGEND

==== Traditional Ojibwe marriage

=·=·= Catholic marriage

| Children born from any of the above unions

¦ Adopted children

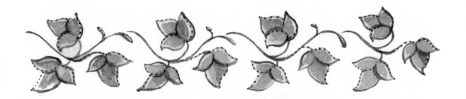

Four Souls

ONE

The Roads

Nanapush

*F*LEUR TOOK the small roads, the rutted paths through the woods traversing slough edge and heavy underbrush, trackless, unmapped, unknown and always bearing east. She took the roads that the deer took, trails that hadn't a name yet and stopped abruptly or petered out in useless ditch. She took the roads she had to make herself, chopping alder and flattening reeds. She crossed fields and skirted lakes, pulled her cart over farmland and pasture, heard the small clock and shift of her ancestors' bones when she halted, spent of all but the core of her spirit. Through rain she slept beneath the cart's bed. When the sun shone with slant warmth she rose and went on, kept walking until she came to the iron road.

The road had two trails, parallel and slender. This was the path she had been looking for, the one she wanted. The man who had stolen her trees took this same way. She followed his tracks.

She nailed tin grooves to the wheels of her cart and kept going on that road, taking one step and then the next step, and the next. She wore her makizinan to shreds, then stole a pair of boots off the porch of a farmhouse, strangling a fat dog to do it. She skinned the dog, boiled and ate it, leaving only the bones behind, sucked hollow. She dug cattails from the potholes and roasted the sweet root. She ate mud hens and snared muskrats, and still she traveled east. She traveled until the iron road met up with another, until the twin roads grew hot from the thunder and lightning of so many trains passing and she had to walk beside.

The night before she reached the city the sky opened and it snowed. The ground wasn't frozen and her fire kept her warm. She thought hard. She found a tree and under it she buried the bones and the clan markers, tied a red prayer flag to the highest branches, and then slept beneath the tree. That was the night she took her mother's secret name to herself, named her spirit. Four Souls, she was called. She would need the name where she was going.

The next morning, Fleur pushed the cart into heavy bramble and piled brush over to hide it. She washed herself in ditch water, braided her hair, and tied the braids together in a loop that hung down her back. She put on the one dress she had that wasn't ripped and torn, a quiet brown. And the heavy boots. A blanket for a shawl. Then she began to walk toward the city, carrying her bundle, thinking of the man who had taken her land and her trees.

She was still following his trail.

Far across the fields she could hear the city rumbling as she came near, breathing in and out like a great sleeping animal. The cold deepened. The rushing sound of wheels in slush made her dizzy, and the odor that poured, hot, from the doorways and windows and back porches caused her throat to shut. She sat down on a rock by the side of the road and ate the last pinch of pemmican from a sack at her waist. The familiar taste of the pounded weyass, the dried berries, nearly brought tears to her eyes. Exhaustion and longing filled her. She sang her mother's song, low, then louder, until her heart strengthened, and when she could feel her dead around her, gathering, she straightened her back. She kept on going, passed into the first whitened streets and on into the swirling heart of horns and traffic. The movement of mechanical, random things sickened her. The buildings upon buildings piled together shocked her eyes. The strange lack of plant growth confused her. The people stared through her as though she were invisible until she thought she was, and walked more easily then, just a cloud reflected in a stream.

Below the heart of the city, where the stomach would be, strange meadows opened made of stuff clipped and green. For a long while she stood before a leafless box hedge, upset into a state of wonder at its square shape, amazed that it should grow in so unusual a fashion, its twigs gnarled in smooth planes. She looked up into the bank of stone walls, of brick houses and wooden curlicued porches that towered farther uphill. In the white distance one mansion shimmered, light glancing bold off its blank windowpanes and turrets and painted rails. Fleur blinked and passed her hand across her eyes. But then, behind the warm shadow of her fingers, she recovered her inner sight and slowly across her face there passed a haunted, white, wolf grin.

3

*　　*　　*

SOMETIMES an old man doesn't know how he knows things. He can't remember where knowledge came from. Sometimes it is clear. Fleur told me all about this part of her life some years after she lived it. For the rest, though, my long talks with Father Damien resulted in a history of the great house that Fleur grinned up at that day. I pieced together the story of how it was formed. The priest and I sat long on the benches set against my little house, or at a slow fire, or even inside at the table carefully arranged on the linoleum floor over which Margaret got so particular. During those long conversations Father Damien and I exchanged rumors, word, and speculation about Fleur's life and about the great house where she went. What else did we have to talk about? The snow fell deep. The same people lived in the same old shacks here. Over endless games of cards or chess we amused ourselves by wondering about Fleur Pillager. For instance, we guessed that she followed her trees and, from that, we grew convinced that she was determined to cut down the man who took them. She had lived among those oak and pine trees when their roots grew deep beneath her and their leaves thick above. Now he lived among them, too, only he lived among them cut and dead.

Here is how all that I speak of came about.

During a bright thaw in the moon of little spirit, an Ojibwe woman gave birth on the same ground where, much later, the house of John James Mauser was raised. The ridge of earth was massive, a fold of land jutting up over a brief network of lakes, flowing streams, rivers, and sloughs. That high ground was a favorite spot for making camp in those original years before settlement, because the water drew game and from the lookout a person could see waasa, far off, spot weather coming or an enemy traveling below. The earth made chokecherries from the woman's blood spilled in the grass. The baby would be given the old name Wujiew, Mountain. After a short rest he was tied onto his mother's back and the people moved on, moved on, pushed west.

From that direction, the place where the dead follow after their names, came wheat in a grasshopper year, hauled out green and fermenting to feed the working crews. A city was raised. Gakaabikaang. Place of the falls. Wood framed. Brick by brick. The best brownstone came from an island in the deep cold northern lake called Gichi gami. The ground of the island had once been covered with mammoth basswood that scented the air over the lake, for miles out, with a swimming fragrance of such supernal sweet innocence that those first priests who came to steal Ojibwe souls, penetrating deeper into the heart of the world, cried out not knowing whether God or the devil tempted them. Now the island was stripped of trees. The dug quarry ran a quarter mile in length. From below the soil, six-by-eight blocks were drilled and hand-cut by homesick Italians who first hated the state of Michigan and next Wisconsin and felt more lost and alien the farther they worked themselves into this country. Every ten hours, night and day, the barge arrived for its load and the crane at the water's edge was set into operation. The Italians slept in shifts and were troubled in their dreams, so much so that one night they rose together in a storm of beautiful language and walked onto the barge to ride along with their own hewn rock toward the farthest shore—forfeiting wages. Still, there was more than enough brownstone quarried, cut, hand-finished, shipped, and hauled uphill, for the construction of the house to continue.

And to the north, near yet another lake and to the edge of it, grew oak trees. On the whole continent and to each direction these were judged the finest that could be obtained. In addition, it proved easy and profitable to deal with the Indian agent Tatro, who won a personal commission for discovering that due to a recent government decision the land upon which those trees grew was tax forfeit from one Indian, just a woman—she could go elsewhere and, anyway, she was a troublemaker. There was no problem about moving the lumber crews right in and so the cut was accomplished speedily. Half was sold. The other, and the soundest of the wood, was processed right at the edge of the city to the specifications of the architect.

Watching the oak grain emerge in warm swirls of umber, the architect thought of several gestures he could make—the sleek entrance, the complicated stairwell, the curves. He saw the wood accomplishing a series of glowing movements in grand proportions. He pointed out the height of imposing windows to Miss Polly Elizabeth, the sister-in-law of his client and now his self-appointed decorating assistant. She took detailed notes and dispatched a servant to the Indian missions to procure fine lace produced by young women whose mothers had once worked the quills of porcupines and dyed hairs of moose together into intricate clawed flowers and strict emblems before they died of measles, cholera, smallpox, tuberculosis, and left their daughters dexterous and lonely to the talents of nuns.

Copper. Miskwaabik. Soapstone. Slate for the roof shingles. A strange, tremendous crystal of pyrite traded from a destitute family in the autumn of no rice. The walls were raised and fast against them a tawny insulation of woven lake reeds was pressed tight and thickened by three layers, and then four, so that no stray breeze could enter. The chimneys were constructed of a type of brick requiring the addition of blood, and so, baked in the vicinity of a slaughterhouse, they would exude when there was fire lighted a scorched, physical odor. Iron for the many skeleton keys the house would take, for the griddles, the handles of the mangle, for the locks themselves, the Moorish-inspired turned railings of the entrance and the staircase, was mined on the Mesabi Range by Norwegians and Sammi so gut-shot with hunger they didn't care if they were trespassing on anybody's hunting ground or not and just kept on digging deeper, deeper into the earth.

Water from the generous river. Fire trembling in beehive kilns. And sweat, most of all sweat from the bodies of men and women made the house. Sweating men climbed the hill and set the blocks and beveled the glass and carved the details and set down floors of wood, parquet, concrete, and alabaster. Women coughed in the dim basements of a fabric warehouse sewing drapes and dishcloths and hemming fine linen. One day overhead a flight of sandhill cranes passed low enough to shoot and the men on the crew brought down nearly a hundred to pluck and roast, eat, digest, and use up making more sweat, laying bricks. A lynx was killed near the building site. One claw was set in gold and hung off the watch fob of John James Mauser, who presented his wife with a thick spotted muff made to the mold of her tender hands. She referred to it ever after as "our first housecat," and meowed at him a little, when they were alone, but she was much too well brought up to do more than that and stiffened harder than the iron banisters when she was touched. Trying to make love to her was for young Mr. Mauser like touching the frozen body of a window mannequin whose temples, only, whitened and throbbing, showed the strain. One night, he looked down at Placide Armstrong Gheen, Placide Mauser. Her arms were stiffly cocked and raised, her legs sprawled, her face as he formed an apology in panic was lean and mournful and suddenly gopherlike. When she curled her upper lip her long front teeth showed, she was like a meek animal mad with fear. He fell back, turned away. He'd married Placide for money, maybe worse, and now they had this house.

They had this house of chimneys whose bricks contained the blood of pigs and calves so that a greasy sadness drifted in the festive rooms. They had this house of tears of lace constructed of a million tiny knots of useless knowledge. This house of windows hung with the desperations of dark virgins. They had this house of stacked sandstone colored the richest clay-red and lavender hue. Once this stone had formed the live heart of sacred islands. Now it was a fashionable backdrop to their ambitions. They had this house of crushed hands and horses dropping in padded collars and this house of the shame of Miss Polly Elizabeth Gheen's inability to sexually attract the architect and the architect's obsession with doorways curving in and curving out and how to get them just exactly so, eminently right. They had this house of railroad and then lumber money and the sucking grind of eastern mills. This house under which there might as well have been a child sacrificed, to lie underneath the corner beam's sunk sill, for money that remained unpaid for years to masons and to drivers was simple as food snatched outright. In fact, there is no question that a number of people of all ages lost their lives on account of this house.

That is the case, always, with great buildings and large doings. Placide knew this better than her husband, but both were nonplussed, and felt it simply was their fate to have this house of German silver sinks and a botanical nursery, of palm leaf moldings and foyers that led into foyers of pale stained glass, this house of bathrooms floored with quiet marble, gray and finely veined. This house of lead plumbing that eroded minds. This house of beeswaxed mantels and carved paneling, of wooden benches set into the entryway wall and cornices and scrolls and heavy doors hung skillfully to swing shut without a sound—all this made of wood, fine-grained, very old-grown, quartersawn oak that still in its season and for many years after would exude beads of thin sap—as though recalling growth and life on the land belonging to Fleur Pillager and the shores of Matchimanito, beyond.

TWO

The Keyhole

Polly Elizabeth

O N   T H E   M O S T exclusive ridge of the city, our pure white house was set, pristine as a cake in the window of a bakery shop. High on sloped and snowy grounds, it was unshadowed yet by trees. The roof, gables, porch, all chiseled and bored in fantastic shapes, were frosted with an overnight fall of gleaming snow. Clipped in cones and cubes, the shrubs were coated with the same lacquer, as was the fountain, frozen, and the white cast-iron lacework of the benches and the tea tables in the yard. The white deer at the gate, dusted with a sugar powder, pawed delicately at its pedestal and nosed the glittering air. The sun was high, small, its brilliance concentrated on this patch of royal blankness, which is why I imagine her arrival from an outside vantage, although I was within.

I see her walking up the pale drive constructed for the approach of a carriage (but what would she know of formal conveyance?). I see the negative of her as she stooped to her dark bundle, the image of a question mark set on a page, alone. Or like a keyhole, you could say, sunk into a door locked and painted shut, the deep black figure layered in shawls was more an absence, a slot for a coin, an invitation for the curious, than a woman come to plead for menial work.

If only I'd had the sense to understand the lay of the situation, instead of the appearance of her—closed, shabby, clean, dark, and dull—I would have noticed we'd met, because of her stubborn and shuttered incomprehension, in the parlor, where social equals gather. We should have conducted our very first conference in one of the rooms out back of the house, reserved for utilities and duty. Instead, Fleur Pillager stood with head bowed before me, dripping on the interlocked figures of the Persian carpet. Azure and indigo, rose-brick and barley pale. I cared for that carpet with a mother's tenderness. A damp cloth to sponge the mud up would be required, I thought, and asked her to discard her boots.

Barefooted, removed from the deceptive brilliance, Fleur was a cipher, a sorry-looking piece of flotsam, I thought, in her coarse brown sack. She didn't even own a proper shawl or a coat, this woman, when she came to us. Desperate, deserted by my Irishwoman the day before (and drubbed low, insulted, she threw my own money in my face!), I hired Fleur Pillager for the laundry, gave to her in the bargain a pair of shoes and the promise of a new-made uniform.

Who could have known?

She would come into the house and before a day was over she would unbow her shoulders and stand up straight. She would look so very different. Who could have guessed that brother-in-law would be sitting in his wooden steamer chair out in the conservatory, and she'd pass by with a bucket in her hands? They would glance at each other, turn away, and look again. I thought her stupid, quite harmless, much quieter than the Irishwoman. I was trying to spare brother-in-law's nerves, as well. I was pleased that this Indian woman had no family connections. Nothing in the look of her and the ignorant silence told me she could possibly end up connected to me.

My brother-in-law, John Mauser, was the cause and perpetrator—I should say the victim as well, though he surely would not countenance that statement. After his war year, my brother-in-law had acquired a specific and demanding need for fresh-pressed clean linen. He sweat, to put it indelicately. Sweat. Once, twice, then three or four times a night, his man-nurse, Fantan, was required to change him from the soaked skin out, to strip the bed down and make it up fresh, with sheets starched smooth and scented with sandalwood. Then, and only then, could my brother-in-law fall asleep. It got to be so we couldn't keep up with the demand. And although quite a number of doctors had attempted to solve the riddle of his symptoms, their lack of progress in other matters quite convinced me that, in regard to this problem, looking to the future was wisest. The sweating would be permanent. And so I was anxious to hire. I wanted a woman specifically to launder, to live in the basement and use the soapstone tubs and iron taps to scald and renew the sheets as Fantan carted them down, and up, and down again from my brother-in-law's closed chamber.

"Good," she answered, when I had explained the position.

"I'm most pleased." I conveyed my satisfaction with professional rigor, although inside I was vastly relieved. I asked how soon she might be able to begin.

"Now," she said.

The emphatic answer filled me with hope. Though she spoke almost not at all, the fact that she understood English was thereby established. Also, the linen had collected. Below my feet, in the basement, a pile that would have scorched my mother's heart lay twisted and towering over the scrub boards and wringers.

"We have a hot water heater and pump, a Maytag, a system that Mrs. Testor will teach you to use."

I offered a proper sum of payment, to which she nodded. Then I told her that although she might hear Fantan occasionally address me by my Christian name, and although out of acceptance of his mental infirmity I'd given up correcting him every time he did so, I absolutely required that she address me as Miss Gheen.

Again, she nodded. How much she understood, I cannot tell. I pointed to myself, tapping my chest.

"Miss Gheen, not Elizabeth."

"Not Elizabeth," she repeated, looking straight into my eyes. *Not Elizabeth* it was after that.

I SUPPOSE it was my fault, then, for not being more specific, but the look she gave me wasn't covered in Miss Katherine Hammond's courses on the hiring and retaining of help. I could not in honesty have categorized the gaze as impertinence, a thing to be dealt with in a spirit of "calm, firm dispatch." None of Fantan's melancholy or Mrs. Testor's occasional sneers were evident. Perhaps it is true that Indians are unintelligible, to the civilized mind I mean, as far removed in habit of thought and behavior as wild wolves from bred

hounds. That comparison is one my brother-in-law made, to opposite effect I believe, when speaking of the people among whom he
lived in the northern wilds for a time in his youth. Although, as I've
since learned, he plundered their land and took advantage of young
women, he still had a higher opinion of their intellect and capac-
ities than I. Soon enough, my views on their talents—for duplic-
ity at least—would change.

The pupil so dark it matched the iris. The gaze a steady beam
that shook the air between us with a subtle motion. It was a curious feeling, almost as though I'd been gazed upon by a predator
and assessed. Through a strong cage, however. I was once again
in charge. As Mother would have, I turned and swept out the massive door expecting her to follow, her in her wood-smoke tatters,
her with that piteous bundle. By Monday morning I could order
a uniform made up for her. A black dress. An apron, with pinstripes,
small gussets, a bow to be tied just so at the small of her back.

Past the kitchen and pantry, past Mrs. Testor, whose eyes flicked
back and forth at the sight of my captive. Mrs. Testor clapped at
her bosom with one raw pink hand as though to beat back a flut-
tering bird. We descended. A pleasant stairway led to the base level
of the house, a feature of our dwelling in which Mother took her
pride. You see, it was her absolute conviction that from the ground
up details mattered. She never did things simply for appearance.
The interfacing of a dress, the trimmed hem, the well-organized
interior of a closet, the underpinnings of a cake. Fresh ingredients,
pristine undergarments, a cellar so clean and light it was a pleasure, no, really, an honor for our help to live there, these were things
important to the late Demeter Hewes Gheen. She always had the
tires of our automobile washed before an important engagement
in town. Before a gathering in our own house, she had the backs

of the clocks and the hung portraits dusted upstairs, even in rooms no one would visit. Down here, the rough stone walls, whitened with a lime base paint, sparkled in the slanting sheets of sun admitted by the generous windows built into the foundation. The floor was brick, laid with runners cut from old carpet.

"Mind the steam pipes," I said, pointing out the scalding copper pipes that ran from the boilers and climbed up two, three floors to the topmost encircled little tower, where Placide maintained her artist's studio. "No touch"—I gestured, wrung my finger, made a face—"very hot!"

Her face grew solemn, as though she understood.

"*Voilà!*" I opened a small, thick door. "Your living quarters."

She was gratified, I could see right off, manifestly pleased by what she saw. The room was austere but comfortable, peaceable and pleasantly dim. The bedding, several blankets deep, boasted not one but two pillows, and a quilt. Beside the bed, not that she'd make use of it for its intended purpose, stood a writing table, the shut drawer containing a Bible, and an old-fashioned lamp with beads and tassels. A cushioned chair, the rose-patterned sleeves polished thin with use, took up a corner. There was a window through which, as we looked up, we saw the face of Fantan, absorbed and serene, as he stooped to briefly watch us.

"We'll just draw these little curtains," I said, running my hand along the brass rod. "Don't you mind him!"

But Fantan's interest did not cause the slightest wobble of composure in this Pillager woman, who smoothed one long-fingered dark hand along the quilt and then deposited her bundle at the baseboard—where her head would rest, according to Mrs. Testor's later testimony, as in Fleur's mind the bed was incorrectly situated.

*   *   *

16

A SCENE, days later. I am posing for my sister, who is painting me as Nebuchadnezzar. To oblige her talent I have taken on hosts of mythological disguises over the years, and her studio is filled with my representation and figure in classical and biblical settings. She is working on a large-scale triptych called *Knowledge and Godlessness*, in which my face appears as almost every scowling pagan from Marx to Salomé, "occluded by veils." Mother was Semiramus. I am desperate to scratch my chin.

"I must see to this new laundry woman." My fingers steal beneath the gray horsehair beard of the troubled hesiarch.

"Your crown! You've tipped it! I wanted it just so," scolds Placide. She wears her dark blond hair smooth to the head, in a simple cut, so as not to detract from what Katherine Hammond called "the purity of brow." It was thirteen years ago, at Miss Hammond's school, that Placide first began to realize her vocation. Painting china plates was how it started. Now, each Wednesday and Friday at noon, the painting teacher comes from the university and the two seclude themselves for hours, engrossed in an intense exploration of form and color.

"I'm tired. I have so much to do."

"Oh well, *then*." Placide bites back on her words, as if to tell me that I have once again shown my true philistine stripe, my low valuation of her talent. She thinks of very little other than the unfolding of this fascinating side of herself, this vibrational urge, as she calls it. Brother-in-law, who makes no secret of his opinions, who called Miss Hammond's vital lessons on deportment "simpering instructions," and referred to my mother's discriminations and opinions as "one long swoon of platitudes," makes short shrift of the painting teacher and the efforts of Placide. I have tried to make up for his lack of kindness by remaining still for hours, sometimes in the most excruciating attitudes, but nothing quite replaces a husband's approval.

"Go, go," says Placide, weary and absorbed.

I pull off the beard, put the paste crown in its hatbox, and am just about to untie brother-in-law's quilted satin smoking jacket when I hear a sort of low howling begin, muffled and irregular. It issues from the south side of the house, the glass porch where brother-in-law sits on fine mornings and takes the strengthening light. I am up in a flash, racing downstairs for the opium bottle. My sister's husband has little physical reserve left these days, and I must dole the medicine out according to the doctor's orders. Fantan would simply pour the stuff down his throat and keep him stupefied, as in fact the poor man wishes. I am more judicious. At these times, all through my brother-in-law's wasted limbs a kind of electrical fury proceeds, each nerve connected and lit up, each muscle pinched and bound. His suffering is a mystery, positively terrible to watch. He flails and runs at the mouth. He loses consciousness, whimpers like a baby or whines, and by the crablike force of his convulsed limbs makes his way under furniture, hides where he can. We believe he suffers from a neuralgia, perhaps the hitherto undetected result of deadly chlorine gas, worsening over the months.

I am, to my mind, adept at dealing with brother-in-law though he always seems to hate the fact that I've seen him and touched him in his state rather than allowing Fantan to administer the medicine. There is no doubt he'll fly into a rage at me, later, but I've locked the medicine away in a drawer just to be sure it isn't given on the sly. In that, my mother failed. She should have made certain long ago that brother-in-law's deterioration was monitored—

not by that strange and sorry scarecrow, but by herself. Since I've taken over brother-in-law's treatment, Fantan says he's worse, but I say that's the illusive quality of progress. Things always seem grimmest before they vastly improve. I walk into the solarium with the bottle and the spoon, but I am met with an unexpected sight. Speechless for a moment, I can do no more than stare.

It is the savage woman I've recently hired to scrub clothes, bent over brother-in-law, I don't know how to say it, like some kind of bird. Hawk-winged and territorial, her brown skirt spread, the apron bows starched and peaked in the back like a cocked white tail, she has him laid out flat. She's working him over, each limb. Obviously, somehow, she has quieted an arm and a leg on one side of him and now she is kneading on his thigh like the dough of a bread. His left arm pounds monotonously on the parquet tiles, beating out a rhythm I fear will break the bone until she catches the wrist and then with no waste in motion seems to wring the muscles smooth in one twist, like squeezing dry a shirt, so that all of a sudden he is calm and limp. His breath floods in and out of his chest, one huge sigh then another, and now Fantan, kneeling at my brother-in-law's head, carefully opens the jaw and removes his own two thick, purpled fingers. He has thrust them between the teeth in lieu of a rolled cloth, for fear that in the throes of his spell my brother-in-law should bite off his own tongue.

I stand there with the bottle and spoon in my hand, quite useless, allowing the scene to resolve itself. It is over. But as I look at the back of her, at Fantan, at the heavy and relaxed form between them, words form against the inside of my skull. I can see them. They make no sense and yet compel me with their vehemence.

Polly Elizabeth, I read, *you've been hoaxed.*

THREE

Medicine

Nanapush

I SHARED WITH Fleur the mysterious self-contempt of the survivor. There were times we hated who we were, and who we had to become, in order not to follow those we loved into the next world. We grew hard. We became impenetrable, sparing of our pity. Sorrows that leveled other people were small to us. We made no move to avoid pain. Sometimes we even welcomed it—we were clumsy with knives, fire, boiling water, steel traps. Pain took our minds off the greater pain that was the mistake that we still existed.

We had only the barest sympathy for those who brought our losses upon us. So when she saw the anguish of the white man, Mauser, that day, Fleur did not rush to him out of a merciful heart.

Though she swooped down in her dress with the stiff white apron wings, she did not descend to save him like an angel of zhaaginaash hope. She gathered the man to herself and fixed his thrashing limbs, smoothed the boil of his tortured blood, pried his fists open, and unstuck his tongue from the back of his throat. But she did these good things for her own benefit, not his. As she helped the cook and the manservant drag him to his bed where the sister proceeded to tie him, she thought of what she might make of that malleable substance, his suffering. How she could benefit herself.

"He must be immobilized!" the sister cried out, her jaws locked in a frenzy of righteousness. "Immobilized at once!"

The woman seemed fond of the word, as Fleur described it, and she used it constantly and made the most of it, dragging out the long *o* and allowing her voice to tremble on each syllable. Elizabeth used strips of cotton sheeting, bandages that she'd had Fleur tear to a precise length and then stitch with a rolled hem. Fastening the man into the bed was evidently a task that this sister accomplished with a certain pleasure. First, she fussed over the neatness of the ties and she tested the knots with a motherly frown. She plucked at the taut strips to make certain they gave the right pressure. After rounding the bed several times to measure her work, she lifted the eyelid of her brother-in-law with a pale, curved thumb. Then she made her mistake. With officious concern, she put her finger underneath his nose to ascertain that he still drew breath. When her hand passed before his mouth, he snapped at it from below the surface of his consciousness and caught her thumb neatly as a fish grabs a fly. He sank a tooth deep. Hell-shrieks! The sister's lungs blasted an eerie steam whistle and the great round woman who did the cooking barged in.

The cook seated herself directly on top of the poor man and pinched his nose shut. Which did nothing, as he breathed through his clenched teeth and through the blood of the howling sister, who beat upon him with a failing vigor until at last she collapsed in a dead faint over the cook's lap, her finger still caught.

At that point, Fleur, who had watched the commotion with amused interest, took charge once again. She untied the bindings with a few sharp movements and pushed back the heavy cook with one hand. She extracted the torn finger of the sister and set her, also, to one side. At once, the cook enlisted the manservant's assistance in carrying the sister to her room. Fleur was left alone with John James Mauser, who suddenly took note of her and narrowed his eyes.

"Anishinaabekwe, na?" he inquired, though exhausted.

She was silent, hiding her surprise. She wondered immediately why a man like Mauser might know her language. But Fleur didn't wonder hard enough. She had an arrogance that held her mind back. Otherwise she might have got the story right there, from the beginning. If she'd only asked, got him talking, he might have spilled his sorry history. I could have told her that Mauser got his start where he ended up—with the trees. I could have told her how he took advantage of one loophole and then another. How in his earliest days, handsome and clever, he had married young Ojibwe girls straight out of boarding school, applied for their permits to log off the allotment lands they had inherited. Once their trees were gone he had abandoned his young wives, one after the next.

That didn't happen on our reservation, but I'd heard of it from others. The Ojibwe absorbed the children he left behind. They

23

became us, not him. The young girls he had left went on to marry other men, but he took the sweetness of their youth just as he stripped off the ancient pine from their lands. Stumps and big bellies was all he left behind. I could have given the story to Fleur, but she never told me where she was going, never asked my advice. So although she was suspicious of his familiarity, she never got at the truth of John James Mauser until it was too late. Of course, it probably would not have mattered what an old man said. She was that dedicated to the shape of her plan.

Fleur began to heal John James Mauser in secret. She burned sweet grass and sage to cleanse the air in his room, gave him swamp tea to purify his blood. Then she began to work on his arms and legs, smoothing them from the inside. After his deep fits his muscles had clenched and contorted, and then froze that way. Fleur learned how to undo the body with a violent kindness of touch. Her fingers were immensely strong. Her grip a steel probe. She unlatched his shoulders and neck. Bit by bit, she untied his cramped muscles, his locked and tortured limbs. She tapered him off the medicines they had been giving him, and his mind cleared. As the constant pain lessened, as Mauser sipped the strong teas and the new Anishinaabeg mashkiki she brewed, he himself might have wondered, after all, why?

There is a simple explanation: when Fleur saw how Mauser already suffered, she felt cheated of her revenge. She wanted the man healthy so that she could destroy him fresh.

FROM THE bottom of the house, Fleur listened up through its pipes and registers. She got to know the house that way, became familiar with every sound that humans could make, and so knew, from her little room at the base, all that was happening above. She traced the sly, masked gait of Fantan and the firm, prideful steps of Polly Elizabeth. She knew the sister's dreamy slide, that wife of Mauser's whom she hardly ever encountered, and then there was the broad footfall belonging to the cook, and at last the agonized, slow, lost creak of Mauser's progress as he made his way from one room to the next though not, as he had before, seated in a wicker-woven wheelchair with metal and rubber wheels. No, after he began Fleur's treatments and continued them, he was at least on his feet.

Once he stood, something happened to the configuration of the household. Before, he had been content to be manipulated in his pain, dragged here, dragged there, set in the window like a plant. Once he stood, he began, almost without anyone noticing it at first, to direct the energy of the household. This direction was accomplished mainly through the leaving of things in new places. Before, everything was taken from him when he finished with it, given to him when he asked for it, controlled. Now he was apt to fetch things for himself and replace them where he pleased. And although this may seem like a small thing, it was in fact a very large thing that he did. For he was unpredictable now—he could be here, he could be anywhere. And the objects he left and was able to reach often surprised people and put them on guard. It had been much easier for everyone, of course, when he was a paralyzed lump.

Now Mauser might be found in the library, at a table, one end of which was spread with his business papers. He muttered and fiercely cracked book spines as he paged through ledgers untouched for years. Or he'd surprise the cook tippling good brandy in the kitchen where he'd wandered in search of a heel of bread.

He might be examining a stamp, holding it up with a tweezers so it caught the most intense and clear southern light, scanning it with a magnifying glass. Or he might be settling himself at his correspondence or even doing what looked like mathematical calculations across sheet after sheet of paper. Or he might even give an order or ask for a specific type of food, but what he didn't do yet and what no one expected of him, anyway, was that he take charge. That would happen. Fleur would see to it, and then it would see to her.

ONCE SHE'D memorized the sounds of the house above, Fleur came upstairs and got to know the house the way a hunter knows the woods. Which floorboards creaked and which were silent. Which steps groaned and which held firm. She greased the hinges of the doors and cupboards. She memorized the lay of the house so that she would be able to tread it easily upon the black night of her choosing. Each night she practiced, she roamed. No one knew it. The house obliged her by standing solid, refusing to shift even in the bluster of winds and roiling snow. The house was well made, thus predictable, the mortars set tight between the stones, the wooden interior pinned smoothly wall to floor. Fleur became so adept in her movements and knowledge that she regularly visited the sleepers, even Fantan, and watched them until she knew their habits even to the regularity of snores and the restless gulp of dreams. She marked the petulant tossing of Placide, and the chilly, deathlike stillness of her sister, Elizabeth. The cook growled mountainously with each breath. Though tongueless, Fantan talked in his sleep. Only Mauser stayed awake.

There was a lamp next to his bed. She saw the crack of radiance below the door. Heard the rustle of stiff pages in a book as he turned them, slowly, reading himself through the deepest hours. Sometimes she frowned as she listened, and in utter silence crept to the wall and settled herself in order to ascertain just when he'd sleep. When he would stop reading and douse the light. The answer never varied. He read until dawn. Slept a few gray hours. Woke in a wretched temper and cursed all he saw and knew.

He suffered an excess of self-sympathy—of that much we can be positive.

In a crack of shadow beside his door, night after night, Fleur marked the turning of pages and grew impatient. Restlessness had plagued her ever since she had entered the house. After all, she was used to great spaces and large doings. She missed getting her own meat and medicines, catching her own fish, snaring rabbits and looping the necks of roosting partridge, the repair and upkeep of her cabin, canoe, traps, and gun, and most of all she missed the care of her daughter. In a strange fit of disconnection, she imagined that she longed for Lulu far more than the girl would miss her. After all, school was a child's world, far from all that Fleur knew. Never having gone to such a place, she imagined it consisted of toys, games, play, children shrieking with excitement—all she'd seen of schools were children at recess. So she fell into the trap, like Mauser, of pitying herself. The great and strong, how is it that they can be so feeble in this regard? Sometimes it seems to me that it's the old sodden weaklings like myself who have the least mercy on our own persons. Maybe we expect nothing. Or have been through far too much. Maybe we are just bottomlessly foolish. At any rate those two, one the shadow of a shadow in the hall and the other a shadow also, an imitation of the ruthless man who'd stolen from the world with careless ease, both poised, caught in time.

Time is the water in which we live, and we breathe it like fish. It's hard to swim against the current. Onrushing, inevitable, carried like a leaf, Fleur fooled herself in thinking she could choose her direction. But time is an element no human has mastered, and Fleur was bound to go where she was sent. Maybe in those long nights as she watched the crack of light beneath the door, she had an inkling. She thought revenge was behind that door, and satisfaction. Maybe she began to realize that she was wrong. There was only time. For what is a man, what are we all, but bits of time caught for a moment in a tangle of blood, bones, skin, and brain? She was time. Mauser was time. I am a sorry bit of time myself. We are time's containers. Time pours into us and then pours out again. In between the two pourings we live our destiny.

Though Fleur was immensely disciplined, the wait got to be too much for her. She sank down against the wall one night, still frowning at the band of light that said Mauser was sleepless. Annoyed with everything to do with him and with her situation, she brooded. The sharp anger that kept her wakeful dulled. Her thoughts drifted. She longed for the trusting touch of her daughter, grew angry at the man behind the door, forgot him, ached for her daughter, grew angry at the man again. Felt that self-pity that they both felt, on either side of the door. Finally, resenting that she had to waste her time to take revenge, she fell asleep.

I haven't said this, but she had a tendency to snore.

The snores of a beautiful woman are both ridiculous and somehow moving. I know. Recall, she had lived in my cabin. Slumped in that grand hallway with her face tipped back, unguarded, her skin exquisitely molded over the stern bones, her eyes up-slanted, the bitter perfection of her lips stuck half open, she breathed an even gurgling gnash. Fleur's snores, her self-betrayal, started softly and then increased in volume as she fell deeper into her sleep. Mauser, in his bed of feather down and fancy silk quilts and ruffed pillows, set his book aside. At the sound of the snores, he was alarmed. He imagined that Fantan had come to curl at his door, out of a protective instinct or because he'd had a bad dream himself. Or if not Fantan, perhaps, he thought, one of his old hunting dogs had been mistakenly left out of his plush night kennel and might catch cold on the floor. He turned his light off, and here is why Fleur did not hear him. Mauser also knew precisely where the creaks hid in the floor. He trod his way around the noisy boards when he wished not to rouse Polly Elizabeth. Now he padded to the door in absolute silence, and opened it. As Fleur herself had greased the hinges, the door made no sound. And as it was a night of moon radiance and the light streamed in the window behind him and the windows at either end of the hall, it was easy for Mauser to see at once that the source of the rumbling snores was no worn-out cur, but a woman. A most extraordinary woman—the laundress who'd revived him. Her face caught the light as though it were poured of tarnished silver. Her face was sculpted of the fabulous dark side of a mirror. Or deep water. Or time, as I've said. Her face gave back an idealized reflection and Mauser was caught in it. That strange beauty emitting snorts and whistles. Oblivious. He watched her curiously for a while, and then he suddenly smiled. He shut the door. Crawled back between the covers. She never knew, but here it was. Like a child reaching into the lake and pulling out a fish, like a fish flipping out of the fry pan into a stream that rushes to the lake, like a dog biting randomly and hauling from the air a rump steak, she got her prize. She had caught him in her sleep.

FOUR

Karezza

Polly Elizabeth

*A*s soon as Fleur appeared in the doorway, ready for my inspection, I regretted my impulse to copy for her that uniform from a certain exclusive hotel in the South of France. The black was never meant to set off so tight a waist, nor the peplum to emphasize those narrow-swiveling sly hips. The bodice with its inset of jet ruche and wide, starched white collar—a terrible mistake. Who could have expected it to frame such an elegant throat? And her eagle's grace of collarbone—perfectly! The three-quarters sleeves and tight cuffs gave distinction to her arms. I turned away without a word. I won't mention my choice of the tinted stockings and the shoes—how I regretted the clever, shiny heels! Her feet were too long for fashion, I told myself, walking from the room, and her hands were rough with work. I tried to find comfort in these shortcomings. But what man rejects a woman on the basis of small defects in her hands and feet?

The rains were heavy and the snows worse. Mold grew in the corners of my brain. Grayish days do that to me, when I'm shut in and contemplate my small surround. I've the wit to do more than run this house for my sister, but my face is bleak and martial. I've never married. And here's the worst. I've a soft heart for children, as well as all things small and helpless, and I sometimes weep into my clenched fists for fury that my sister has provided me no nephew or niece. One day I decided, in spite of opposition from all quarters, to obtain a small lady's lapdog—a Pomeranian. A black clever-eyed bit of fluff with sharp teeth and a bitter yap. I imagined myself in some way defined by my relation to another creature. The dog would look elegant when I rode in motorcars, and fit my wardrobe perfectly as I tended to favor contrasting checks and black-and-white plaids. I would be known for my black Pomeranian and there would be a dog, at least, to sleep with me in my bed.

The breeder brought round the complete litter and I chose one at last—it took me just an hour—I picked him for his pleading eyes. Who else, after all, needed me enough to beg?

THOUGH I AM fond of my sister and do not begrudge her the lopsided distribution of comely attributes, I am nevertheless aware of her limitations. Placide was considered scatterbrained, and our tutor had often chastised her, but I've had occasion to wonder whether indeed she was created with a brain at all. In the aftermath of brother-in-law's episode, life resumed a routine serenity, outwardly at least. But I had seen what I had seen. I tried to tell Placide.

"Sister," I addressed her straight out, one morning as I posed for her in pale north light, "your husband has eyes for the laundress."

"She's dark as a Nubian. More to the left. Turn your head. There. Your beard is rippling up on one side and your collar shows."

I smoothed the piece of lamb's wool we'd taped to my chin, and persisted.

"I've a mind to let her go."

"Oh, don't!" This captured my sister's attention. She even set her camel's hair brush down, though she loves to flourish it. "She irons my ribbons!" Placide picked up her brush again and dabbed a minuscule bit of color on her canvas. "And the bedclothes, my underlinen, all the tablecloths and napkins. She gets them so very white, my dear, quite in contrast to her complexion!"

Placide dimpled at me, waiting for me to laugh at her attempted witticism. I did not indulge her.

"Watch out, sister, have a care. He's quite"—I chose the word without thinking how absurd it might sound uttered from beneath a false lamb's wool beard—"*besotted*." The wool got in my mouth and I spluttered to get rid of it.

Placide laughed out loud and shook her thin, dry curls. She wrinkled her nose, a gesture that was charming when she was a girl but which now made her look like a moth-eaten rabbit. She fluffed the silk bow on her painter's smock as much as if to say, What would you know of men and their besottedness?

I do know, I thought, *I can see it*. I know a love crush far better than you do, sister. You vain bit of fluff! Though I would die for you, I suppose, were it to come to that, I do see you clearly. And I know more about the direction of men's desires because I've watched from the outside. I saw how they once looked at you, before everything about you dulled to an aged girl and your hair fell out. Their eyes followed your gestures and their bodies were always half poised, half turned, ready to sidle or leap, crawl or elegantly saunter in your direction whenever you changed your position in a room. You were the sun to their yearning faces, however eagerly they tried to conceal their interest. But it was a blank power. You were thinly wrought, a skim of cream, a pleasing sugar dip. Which is why I worry so intensely now, and fear this servant whose craft took me unaware.

Yet the new woman did such an excellent job that I had absolutely no cause for complaint. Fleur filled and drained the electric tumbler washer, operated the short mangle, and at any time of day, while directing Mrs. Testor, I was apt to hear the thump and dance of her irons from below. The bedding appeared, stacks of it precisely folded and sun-bleached to a marvelous whiteness. In addition, she was discreet. I saw little of her. Fleur never appeared in the kitchen except at mealtimes, and as for the rest of the house, she made her rounds silent as a wraith. I never saw her on any of the other floors although the linens were delivered and changed, precisely as I had instructed, even to the paint smocks for Placide and the hand towels at my dressing table. Brother-in-law seemed both satisfied with the condition of his room and yet completely unaware that Fantan and Mrs. Testor no longer struggled and bickered over what was to be done with the mounds of soiled sheets and wrinkled pajamas that he discarded by the sixes and sevens. I was even lulled, as anyone would be I suppose, into the resumption of a modest social life.

Nothing like life had been, of course, when Mother held sway. She had an unsurpassable gift for organizing formal picnics, sleigh rides, outings of various types. On those rare occasions when she pressed brother-in-law into joining the fun I never shall forget the picture that he and Placide, the two of them, made in spanking white, she on his arm, walking the grounds by the lake as the light turned golden and their shadows dragged beneath their heels like long and languid blue capes. They were really quite magnificent. She was the beauty of the avenue when she married—tall and slim, with a mass of dark golden hair that curled and crackled with lights. He was young too, wealthy, unpredictable, purported to be the son of minor British royalty and a German industrialist, an entrepreneur and scholar whose interests ranged from the classification and study of serpents to the quiet manipulation of investments. I was to find out that his heritage was more than exaggerated, it was a disgraceful lie, although his wealth was not. He was financially unharmed by all market tremors and even benefited from every crisis. He'd acquired a stiff reputation for his handling of the family lumber business and the railroad line, which stretched west from its terminus, went on forever, its print bold and black as doctor's stitches on the maps he had me trace with my fingers.

"Our son could run this, why not?" he used to say, wistfully, to Placide. Of course she had no interest in bearing a son or daughter. When he tried to interest me in his doings, I would politely dip my head. I could no more make out and take fascination in the schemes, the maps, the enthusiasms in his office, the ins and outs, than my sister could allow her body to conceive.

It was a shame, I thought, that Placide and I had not been fused into a single person. I would have done things with her looks, and there's no question that she sorely needed brains. But we were woefully separate and single in our beings. Perhaps if we'd worked together, we could have managed John James Mauser. But too late. Once the laundry woman had begun to exert some sort of influence, my brother-in-law started acting on his own. He actually summoned a doctor who specialized in male diseases. The man made a house call all the way here from Chicago. The famous doctor arrived on a drizzly afternoon and after we took his raincoat, umbrella, rubber galoshes, and a hat away to dry and brush, he was shown upstairs, where he secluded himself with brother-in-law for most of a day.

SEEKING TO enlighten myself on the particulars of brother-in-law's condition, for his own good of course, I was forced to eavesdrop. After the esteemed Dr. Fulmer had finally finished examining his patient, he stepped into the hall where I was sitting, waiting, knitting. I had practically completed two pairs of socks.

"Put down those needles," he glared at me from underneath his little band of black hair. "Are you the wife?"

"No," I answered, though a bolt of conceit pierced me.

"Then fetch the wife!" he ordered.

I went upstairs and, with difficulty, persuaded Placide to leave off detailing the hem of some figure's majestic robe. She followed me downstairs, and I ushered them both into a small sitting room, knowing full well that there was a thin panel in the wall between the two rooms. Through that panel, by means of an ordinary water glass pressed to my ear, I was able to hear the entire conversation so clearly that on several occasions I had to bite my lip so as not to offer correct information. Placide, of course, distracted and immersed in her artistic pursuits, knew less than I of brother-in-law's diet, sleep, taking of the air, and general treatment.

Placide had already hinted to me of her husband's trouble-some spermatorrhea, which he claimed was brought on by the practice of Karezza in the marital relation. So it did not surprise me to hear the doctor question my sister on the specifics of the practice laid out in Dr. Alice B. Stockham's useful book. Placide had confided to me her terror of pregnancy, and I had laid aside my own longings for a nephew or niece in order to preserve Placide's health. I had, of course, meant no harm when I placed the book in Placide's hands, and in fact I still insist that Dr. Stockham's adaptations of Zugassent's practical methods of loving could, if sincerely practiced, improve the relations between the sexes and even save marriages.

"Now I want you to be perfectly open with me, Mrs. Mauser," said Dr. Fulmer. "Can you describe this practice of Karezza to me in exact physical terms?"

Placide, of course, could not. Her modesty was a barrier. She tried her best to convey the spirit of the practice without resort-ing to crude word-pictures.

"We exercise the mutual power of our wills," said Placide. "And the power of the heart."

"For what purpose?"

"To collect and act on loving thoughts."

There was a pause.

"That is all very well," said the doctor. "But insofar as marital congress is concerned . . ."

"We have always practiced a conscious conservation of cre-ative energy." Placide was earnest. "It has had the most exciting effect on my artistic output!"

"I see." The doctor seemed to be taking notes. "Is procreation possible through the marital relationship?"

"It is not wished," said Placide with quiet assurance.

"Well then," the doctor tried again, "is the congress satisfactory?"

"We have attained a marvelous level of mutual reciprocity," said Placide. "And now, if I may excuse myself."

"Not just yet."

I could tell the doctor was not only losing patience but running out of circumlocutions.

"I must inquire, Mrs. Mauser, does the practice of Karezza require the partakees to suppress emission?"

"Yes," said Placide, rather strongly, "there is no crisis!"

"No propagative crisis," said the doctor, making certain.

Placide must have nodded or made some sign, for she gave no verbal answer.

"Then my diagnosis is confirmed." The doctor's tone was rather grim. "The frustration of your husband's natural discharge has resulted, I must say, in the most bitter penalty. Sit down, Mrs. Mauser. You will hear me!"

I heard the chair creak.

"In the beginning," said the doctor, "your husband's dulled eye, his sallow countenance, drawn features, and pained air of melancholy, as well as his insistence on social isolation, caused me to suspect that he suffered from one of the secret diseases."

I gasped, rather loudly, and Placide said nervously, "What was that?"

"A secret disease," repeated Dr. Fulmer, mistaking her suspicion for ignorance. "If I must be completely direct, so be it. I suspected the masked pestilence!"

But Placide must have still affected that blank sweetness one finds so frustrating.

"Gonorrhea!" he practically yelled. My glass shook and I believe I flushed to the roots of my hair. The doctor forged on. "His previous doctor must have suspected the same. For that reason, the patient was prescribed a diet absent of ales or malt liquors, coffee, salt meats, intense seasoning, and asparagus."

"He was given no asparagus," said Placide, meek now.

"For Chordee, which he suffered at night, he was of course advised to place his posterior against a cold wall."

"He did that," said Placide, "as far as I know."

"His manservant also assisted in his nightly treatments."

Placide must again have looked stupefied.

"Prolonged immersion of the"—here Dr. Fulmer struggled, but used the words—"male sexual member in hot water. I believe it was of some benefit. But when your husband did not respond to my colleague's satisfaction, he was prescribed urethral injections of sulfate of zinc. Mrs. Mauser, those treatments had little or no effect. For that reason, I conducted today's frank interview, which enlightened me to the extent that I have changed the diagnosis. Mrs. Mauser . . ." The doctor paused dramatically. "Your husband suffers from a locomotor ataxia and melancholic neuralgia complicated by a rare male chlorosis, all brought on by a damming of the sperm!"

"Oh!" Placide sounded quite shocked.

"Where do you think it goes?" asked Dr. Fulmer, rather savagely. I pictured him leaning forward, into Placide's face, and tapping his head, "To the brain! To the brain!"

"I've heard enough." Placide threw herself toward the door. Her heels skittered on the polished parquet. I quickly set my glass on the table and retreated to a chair, opened some book and pretended for some time to read, at first because I feared one of the two might enter and find me. But their steps retreated down the hall. As I mulled over what I had learned, I remained fixed in place with my eyes locked on the open pages of a book that made no sense, with a title I can't remember. I couldn't help it. Other pictures, other words made me splutter like a child. A laugh kept bursting out of me. I was helpless to hold it back. His posterior against a cold wall! No sooner did I succeed in pushing one picture from my thoughts than I imagined Fantan drawing that basin of hot water. I tried with all my might not to think of the immersion of the male part, but my defense failed. Another laugh assaulted me. I am ashamed to say it was at least half an hour before I could compose my features and calm my nerves sufficiently to leave.

THE LEECHES arrived the next day, an experimental procedure. Dr. Fulmer, his tiny mustache all aquiver, applied them directly to brother-in-law's temples, where they would draw off an excess of fluid produced by the seminal overflow. Although I brought towels and attempted in my way to assist, I was soon barred from brother-in-law's room and had to content myself by directing the preparation of invalid foods. I decided on chicken cream, lemon jelly, and peptonized beef tea. The last I prepared myself. I shredded the beef and set it in a saucepan of cold, salted water. I was heating the mixture gently, stirring out the juice, when Fleur came into the kitchen. Either she didn't see me, or she acted entirely for my benefit.

"Hot water," she ordered Mrs. Testor, setting down a basin next to the stove.

"Hot water yourself," said Mrs. Testor, who was not to be ordered about by the likes of Fleur.

"Hot water!" I exclaimed, shocked that such a mission be entrusted to Fleur. "I hardly think that for you to bring the hot water is appropriate." I shooed her off. For such an intimate procedure, I reasoned as I rushed up with the basin, better that a family member be in attendance.

"Thank you." Dr. Fulmer accepted the basin at the door to brother-in-law's room. I followed him in.

"I need assistance," said Dr. Fulmer over his shoulder. "Will you kindly hold the basin, Miss Gheen? The patient is suffering acute neuralgic spasms characterized by twitching of the extremities. The force of his movements could very well tip the basin. Take the utmost precautions."

I did so. Brother-in-law was sitting on the bed, quite limp, supported by Fantan. The leeches were blackly clustered at his temples and he was taking shallow breaths. His eyes were shut.

"Now put the basin on the floor directly before the patient and kneel there with your hands on the rim, Miss Gheen. Steady!"

Although I felt some trepidation regarding the procedure at this point, I took a deep breath and fiercely counseled myself to show but the most refined sense of disinterested compassion. I knew, of course, the location of the afflicted part. Yet I had not ever actually seen one. I couldn't think how the doctor intended to immerse the necessary member while brother-in-law was in a seated position, but I knelt on the floor anyway. Fantan laid brother-in-law against some pillows, crouched beside me, removed John James Mauser's socks and slippers. He then placed brother-in-law's feet carefully in the basin. At that point I rose and left the room. His feet! I have never liked other people's feet. I must confess it. Even as a girl I would avert my eyes when Placide took off her shoes. I made my way downstairs to the kitchen, wondering just what Dr.

Fulmer took me for—a servant? Spinster handmaiden? My beef tea had boiled to a jelly meanwhile, too dark and rich for a weak constitution.

LATER, as I devoured the beef tea myself, I reflected. I realized that I missed being privy to brother-in-law's treatments. For much of my life I was not acquainted with what may seem the obscure derivation of the adjective "sincere." It is from two Latin words, *sine*, without, and *cera*, wax. What a rare thing it is to be treated *without wax*. My desire is always to conduct relationships based upon honest regard. As I sipped the last drops of beef tea I tried to enumerate moments stripped of pretense and all I could come up with was those efforts of mine, with brother-in-law, when he grasped my hand in desperate gratitude, unknowing, and allowed me to really see him. As I relived those moments of extremity, a strange thought met me unawares. Were I not to know him, or someone, some person, at this radical depth, I fear my time on earth would be hideous. I was surprised to think this. But it crossed my mind that to know others on a superficial level only is a desperate hell and life is worth living only if the veneer is stripped away, the polish, the wax, and we see the true grain of the other no matter how far less than perfect, even ugly, even savage at the heart.

FIVE

Under the Ground

Nanapush

ON THE NIGHT that Fleur
decided it was time to kill James Mauser, she cleaned her knife on
her hair and tested its edge. He was well enough, she thought, he
valued his life sufficiently, to suffer as she took it away. She'd
grown tired of the long wait, and wanted to go home. So she bundled together all that she owned, set it out by the back door, and
slipped like a shadow up the service staircase and down the wide
hall of the main entry. From there to the stairs that led up to the
ballroom. Stairs that didn't creak at all if you trod their edges. She
glided down the upstairs hall to the door of his bedroom. The
dark was a quiet blanket. Everyone was asleep. Turning the crystal doorknob with a stealthy hand, she entered Mauser's bedroom

and stood in the entryway, regarding him. A low lamp burned just beside the man, who slept lightly. A book was splayed open on his chest. Small professorial reading glasses perched half askew on the bridge of his nose. Fleur edged soundlessly close to the bed and, as he turned in his sleep, frowning, sensing her proximity, she nestled close to him as a snake to a warm rock. His frown changed to a dreamy smile. She gently coaxed his head to the pillow of her breast. He groaned happily in his dream and she put her knife to his throat. She woke him by breathing into his ear.

"I have come here to kill you."

"What took you so long," said Mauser. He was not asleep after all. He had been waiting without sleep for many nights on end. He had rehearsed what he would say to her so that he wouldn't tremble, yet he could not control a slight quiver as her knife creased his throat.

"Do you know who I am?" said Fleur.

"Of course I do," said Mauser.

"Who am I?"

"You're a relative of one of the women I wronged." His breath caught as Fleur's knife cut a little deeper.

Her voice thickened with rage. "One of them? Awenen? I am the woman whose land you stole."

Mauser was silent. He'd taken the land of so many it was impossible that he should remember just who they were. His mind was reeling back through titles and false transfers and quitclaim deeds. He thought he'd had her figured. Who could she be?

"Who are you?" he asked, then, very humbly.

Fleur answered in a sarcastic, angry voice. "I am the sound that the wind used to make in a thousand needles of pine. I am the quiet at the root. When I walk through your hallway I walk through myself. When I touch the walls of your house I touch my own face. You know me."

"No, I don't," said Mauser, now thinking that she was crazy and supposing himself to be in even more danger than he had imagined.

"I'm going to slice you open," said Fleur, all in Ojibwe, which she knew well he understood, "and take out your guts and hang them on the walls. Then I'm going back home to live on the land you took. If you send your spirit there to look for me, I'll kill your spirit too."

"I won't send my spirit," said Mauser, "it is meant to serve you."

He was a hardened man, a much different sort of man than the one who presented himself to his wife's family, and to society at large. Still, though he had entertained certain grotesqueries of fate with an unflinching, stoic enjoyment, he was at the moment afraid, on a level that surprised and then embarrassed him. He had the childish urge to wet the bed, and knew that if he did she would immediately slit his throat. Only with the most monumental effort did he keep from pissing. He counted his breaths to keep from thinking about the knife, but could not help imagining that with each one he might have breathed his last. The next, therefore, came as a gift. The air that filled his lungs was refreshingly sweet. A wave of euphoria gripped him at the beginning of each breath and one of terror at its end. His next breath might whistle through the slit in his throat, and that would be the last breath he'd hear. Yet as another and another breath came and went, he grew encouraged. Gradually, he felt the woman's curiosity gain the upper hand.

"How?" she asked, unwillingly. "How is your spirit meant to serve me?"

Now the burden of responsibility for his own life lay with Mauser. If he answered well, he might survive, but if he gave a less than satisfactory destination for his spirit, it would pour fast from the extra smile underneath his chin. His brain raced, and then he spoke.

"My spirit is meant to be the slave of your spirit. I will make you my wife and give you everything I own. And more than that, I will love you no matter what you do to me, as a dog does. My spirit is meant to be g'dai, your animal, to do with as you wish, let live or kill."

Once he'd said this, to his desperate surprise, he knew it was true. He couldn't have known, however, exactly how true. Nor how painful would be the living out of his original apprehension. He only knew at that moment the fabulous relief as her hand lifted away from his throat. And then the shift of her body told him she was considering something else. He hadn't a notion in the world that it would have been easier for him if she'd used her knife.

OF COURSE, as she was Four Souls, she probably knew all that would happen in some way unavailable to us. Pillagers don't do anything without a reason, though it is sometimes hidden even to them. I don't hold with everything people say about Fleur's people, but I have seen what I've seen. When Fleur took the name Four Souls she thought she was taking a name that would build her up, protect her, and it was true, the original Four Souls was a powerful woman. What Fleur didn't know was the name would take over and have more of an effect upon her than she could

have conceived. For the name was something else—it was force-
ful, it was old, and it had its own intentions. In the end, it was
even stronger than Fleur.

There are names that go on through the generations with calm
persistence. Names that heal a person just for taking them, and
names that destroy. Names that travel, names that bring you home,
names you only mutter in the deep water of your sleep. Names that
bring memory of painful attachments and names lost to time and
the reckonings of chance. Names are throwaway treasures. Names
hold the sweetness of youth, bring back faces and unsettling resem-
blances. Names acquire their own life and drag the person on their
own path for their own reasons, which we can't know. There are
names that gutter out and die and then spring back, distinguished.
Names that go on through time and trouble, names to hold on your
tongue for luck. Names to fear. Such a name was Four Souls.

So the name was going to do what it wanted with Fleur Pillager.
From the beginning, she did not own it. Once she took it, the name
owned her. It would slam her to the earth and raise her up, it would
divide her, it would make her an idiot and nearly kill her, and it
would heal her once it had finished humbling her. Four Souls—
the original Four Souls, I mean—had exactly what her name tells
us, four souls that she could use. Four times she knew in her life
that within the year she was meant to die, and so, those four times,
she threw out a soul. That soul went about as a bird or animal, the
shape of which only she knew. That soul roamed here and there,
gaining knowledge of things, then came back and reported to its
owner. So Four Souls grew wiser. But she knew too much already,
perhaps, as those Pillagers do. For she was the daughter of a
woman who became a healer when she was only a girl.

I'm going to lay down the roots here. I'm going to explain things. This is where the story fills in deeper, where you see through the past so you understand what made Fleur and the name she took too powerful to contain. This, I suspect, is the shadow Fleur dragged out behind her when she was born. This is the face she wore on her face. For she was born with a spirit face on her face and that face was laid away in the woods for the Gizhe Manito to love and to name. That face had a name but we don't know it. We would never understand it. That face was named in the spirit language. Fleur got her name, her pretty French name, from a trapper's wife, but of course she had the name that no one could speak. And when she took the Four Souls name, she brought down on herself not only the great strength, but the sorrow and the complexity of the woman who came before.

IN THE TIME before the time the last treaty came about, there was a great healing that took place in the camp of Under the Ground. It made us weep, it made us sorry, it made us wonder who we are. It made confusion between the dead and the living, this world and the other alongside our ordinary life. And yet, in spite of those conflicts, what happened that night gave slender hope on the reservation land that the old ones called ishkonigan, leftover, scraps so poor even the greediest would cast these bits aside.

The mother of the girl who became the one we know as Four Souls was born upon the great red island, fourth daughter of a fourth daughter in a line of dawn woman healers going back across the miigis water and farther yet, back before the oldest remember. Everybody who met her face-to-face thought her a simple woman—small, short, and round with a capturing smile. Her eyes, they might be penetrating when they wanted to know your case, but otherwise they had no other symptom in them but kindness. Nevertheless, she had accomplished something few understood.

As it happened, disease struck. Some left old sacred ground, struck out for the new, hearing some fresh powerful tale of the men in black robes who did not copulate. Besides cures, people needed supplies. Blankets. Knives. Who can blame them? Supposing the world went dead around you and all the animals were used up. The sky, too, of pigeons, doves, herons, and rain. Supposing one new sickness after another came and racked deep, so that young men and women threw themselves on stones to break their limbs in the crush of their fever. Suppose this happened in your own life, what then, would you not think of surrendering to the cross, of leading yourself into the hands of new medicines?

Some did, many did, for a time I was even one. But I came back from the Jesuits with a pair of eyeglasses, six books, a watch, and the old gods still strong in my heart. I am Nanapush. I am the one they call fire, the one who makes my own snare, who shot off a tree branch, ate snakes to survive, had wife upon wife, and remembers the making of Under the Ground.

She took her name when she was still a young girl registered as Fanny. At the loss of her own mother from the welted sickness, she decided, in anger, to go after death itself, and so had herself buried alive in a birch-bark covering. Connected only to the upper world by a breathing straw, she went down into the earth. Four days. Four nights. She decided to search through the layers of the earth. She would search for special help as she descended deeper, deeper. The old men drummed and the women sang to give her courage, but all that they could see from the soft earth of her grave was the tube of rawhide. Passing their hands above the opening not a one of them could tell whether or not she still drew breath.

It was on the fifth dawn they uncovered her, gently, scooping out dirt with their old paws. Singing, they brushed the earth away from her face, blue black and stone hard. They continued. Took the rawhide straw from her lips still frozen in a frowning *o*. Finally lifted her out in her stiff death shape and shook the dirt and beetles and worms from her clothes and hair. She was wearing a red dress and smelled of the beginnings of a powerful decay, a smell of bear, a smell of the dead lashed high in trees, an odor that came and went the rest of her life when she knew she would lose out to her enemy, death.

Niiban, crooned the old ones, *mino ayaa sana,* laying her upon a laced platform of blankets. Sleep and be well, though whether she was dead or living they did not know, not yet, not until during the quiet, slow, washing of her face and arms her eyelids throbbed, her mouth unpinched, and she drew a rough breath.

SO THAT was how she got her power and her name changed from Fanny Migwans into Anamaiiakiikwe, Under the Ground. That was how she got her chance to doctor. She was told the names of plants down there. She cured me once, I remember, of an eyesore sickness that came from rubbing my face after cleaning some fish. She mixed up a pulp of roots by chewing. Spitting, she made a paste of that and tenderly soothed it onto my shut eyelids. I remember her square woman's hands—padded, priestly, warm—her slow calm, her bear's eyes, her grip.

She had no children until she was well into the fourth decade of her life, and then she had a daughter by an Odawa man she loved and who loved her and who came to her house to visit every night. The daughter, you could tell, was the blood of her heart. Warm-eyed, laughing. Under the Ground named her Anaquot, Cloud, raised her close, and took her everywhere, first in a pack trimmed in black velvet that she decorated with beaded flowers and red straps, then alongside her on a small pony, walking slow, then everywhere as though she was her helper in the doctoring. They picked plants, offering tobacco to each one, and they tended their traplines and fished together on the lake. All winter, every day, Under the Ground broke a trail for Anaquot to walk to school. Every night, she brought her daughter home safe through the woods and put her in her own blankets, rolled her tight. They had a garden of squash and beans, and some wild brown chickens, a dog, a stand of chokecherries, and a slough where occasionally Under the Ground took her shotgun and blasted down a duck for her daughter's supper.

This was how they lived until the girl's eleventh full year, when she sickened suddenly, of a disease that had no name and had never been seen before on this reservation ground so that no one knew what to do.

It started as a weakness in the eyes and a tired sorrow, then a low cough that did not get better but deepened until the lungs made pink foam, but then, in the case of Anaquot, six nights of drumming and suck doctoring frightened away the disease so she seemed better all that winter, even cured.

During that time, another child, LaFortier's son, fell in hot coals of the sugaring fire and caught his little shirt in flames, ran in circles until his uncle put it out. This child was laid more dead than living on a blanket at the sugaring camp, and Under the

Ground was fetched. She came quickly, and used a paste on the boy's burnt skin. She then caused the fire to be built up exactly as it was when the child fell in. She talked to that fire and prayed with it. Then she gathered its coals and tamed them in her hands, spoke to them softly, until they did not cause pain to her or to the child they had burned.

The boy healed with only the faintest ripple of scars, but from that time on, Under the Ground's hands were striped by wrinkled gray tissue, bent like a frog's. Yet she never hid her hands away in her apron. She was proud.

During the next winter, though, Anaquot stumbled on the path from school and fell asleep in snow. Her mother found her when the light was almost blue, and carried her home slung across her back, still dreaming in sleep that grew deeper and yet more restless as the night went on. By morning, Under the Ground's eyes burnt and her own limbs loosened and she slept curled around her daughter in terror.

You heal by taking on the pain of others, by going down to argue with death itself, by swallowing the sharp bone and vomiting the sickness out in your own blood. That old woman's daughter lay next to her, close, curled the way she used to lie within her mother's body. The healer ached for her child's return. There was nothing—no act, no murder, no betrayal, no agony—that she was not prepared to accomplish in order to save her girl.

Under the Ground woke to hear unusual noises.

The shadow of a person wanders as though sorry to leave. Touching old possessions—a kettle, a favorite knife. Sometimes a shadow takes a water pail, a dipper, a handful of flour or rice, but it cannot use these things, must drop them, demands attention in that way.

So that is how Under the Ground knew she had some assistance in her work—things dropped, murmurs, low steps all through the night that she lay with her daughter in the blankets.

By morning, worse. Both woke spotted with the girl's blood from coughing. Deep in her chest she heard the slow whine of air escaping. Under the Ground built up the fire and cleaned her daughter. Brought out an old robe, ancient and still smelling of the greenwood smoke. Put Anaquot on it and covered her with blankets.

"Mother, Mother," she said, "N'gah, why have you left me?"

"I'm here," Under the Ground assured, and set about preparing her things.

"Mother, Mother, are you gone yet? Why don't you stay with me?"

"I'm here," wept Under the Ground.

"I'm cold," said her girl.

Under the Ground built the fire higher and hotter. Down the path came an old man who had been thinking about her, who had pots fall in the night too and wondered who might need him. He took along a young nephew, a helper, yawning and annoyed to be awake.

"Sit over there, sit by the western wall," insisted the healer, my uncle. "Death is curious and determined. Death comes from that direction. My boy, be strong and do not let anything get by you."

The door of Under the Ground's house opened to the east, as all our houses did then. Under the Ground brought the water into it and gave some to the old man but not to the helper. To that boy she said, "Go fetch us some more. Make yourself useful." She didn't say it in a rough way, just in a direct way, but still the boy's heart went resentful. He wanted to run off and set snares in the woods, and he would have done that had he not pitied the girl in the blankets. So small, so bleak, so still, like and unlike his own slim sister. He went out, fetched the water, and in the old way his uncle had taught him, chopping away the ice and sinking the bucket in the stream just a little bit against the flow.

I ignored sticks to carve, rabbit paths perfect for snares, tracks of a deer on the path to the house. I tried to concentrate, even to think the way my uncle might, for the daughter of Under the Ground was laboring to breathe.

The old man drummed.

He picked up and drummed. He used a stick carved of sumac, the beater filled with cattail down. His drum was painted with a long yellow stripe.

Into my mind came the smell of fish and new rice, and then the ash smell of new leaves burning and the touch of my mother's hands on my face. I could not stay awake. Sometimes I dozed off but my uncle did not—he drummed all day, but the girl continued to go down.

Under the Ground made a paste of leaves, a paste of nettles, a paste of roots she chewed up and spat, a paste of dead bees. She turned her daughter over with gentle care and she bone-doctored, spat out three fat white ants. They crawled into the fire and burst, lighting thick shadows on our faces. Around halfway through the night, my uncle's voice broke. I took over and sang when Under the Ground bent her head to feel Anaquot's breath on her cheek, its low, strained rasp.

We went on through the next day in a confused haze, and on through the night. By now there was no time and no meaning. Everything had stopped but my uncle's drumming. A terrible odor of burning hair, then a strange fugitive sweetness. Food a relative brought, a pot of meat soup, and still the work. Under the Ground's hair was wild with grease, sweat, and stuck off her shoulders in rigid tails. Her face was harrowed and her eyes sunk and red, tiny with smoke and tears. She'd shrunk and withered on her bones. Her face was bearlike, her snout wide, her eyes deep and dull as nails.

By the third day and night my uncle took me aside, drew me close to him, and whispered, "When you see the old woman go out, open that girl's eyelids and see if she's living yet."

So when Under the Ground went out, drawn by my uncle's call, I went to her daughter. Her cheek was rock cold and her hand stiff as a bundle of sticks. I thumbed her eyelid up. It stayed up and the iris stared into darkness, chilled and fixed. I pressed down the eyelid and crept back into the corner, put my head down when Under the Ground returned. I poked up the fire and the old woman kept praying, now telling her medicine mean things. Threatening her medicine.

"I'll throw you away," she warned. "You're no good to me if you can't help my girl."

She rattled the bag. "Get out of here." She screamed. "I don't want you." She scolded, she grew hard, "I don't want you unless you help me now." She threw down her medicine. Dried plants and small objects went rolling across the dirt and hide piled on the packed earth. I was fully awake now, paralyzed with fright. My uncle's drumming stopped. Even the fire did not dare crackle or shift. In its waiting glow Under the Ground bent to her child and called her in a fearful, soft voice:

"Daughter, daughter . . ."

Under the Ground stropped her knife on her belt. Singing a

wild song I never want to hear again, singing hard and low, then high as a crazy loon, she slashed her arms deeply, four cuts on each arm. The cuts were deep, I saw them. To the bone. The girl moved.

Anaquot sat straight up in the blankets, her hooded eyes still shut. I watched as a smile slowly came across her face, sweet at first, as though she was dreaming, then broader and deeper until it was terrible, a skull's grin. Her eyes flew open and a staring blackness as of the cold place gripped the room.

That is when I saw Under the Ground throw out one of her daughter's souls. Throw it out of her. I saw her grab an animal struggling in the girl's blankets and then she threw it hard at the western wall—through the wall—it was gone—when I looked, and then looked back, the girl had crumpled backward and was peacefully resting.

THAT SOUL stumbled around and got into the body of a white raccoon and for a time it was seen about the edge of the town and on the farms curious and hungry, its eyes full of cunning light. Seemed to us it went around just watching and figuring. Night, the trill it made was a stranger's laugh. Days, we tried to let it go, tried to forget.

And then an old man trapped the white raccoon, found it in his leg-hold trap, dead. He came to my uncle, shaking. He sat at our table. After a time he spoke, told us he had opened it up and the animal was hollow inside. Nothing there. No heart. No lungs. No guts. Just empty.

Some souls keep stumbling the rough paths. Some try to get into their old beds and rooms. Some you see traveling bad, balls of white light, some you pass in the woods with no notice but the prickle on the back of your neck. Some souls return. Some come back to people. After a time they return with more knowledge than they went out with.

Hers came back with all our secrets. Hers came back with a taste for charred bones. Hers came back with the sensitive paws and bright eyes of a healer. Hers came back masked, laughing, with a mouth full of delicate white teeth. Her soul came back knowing too much, saying no word. Hers came back and that daughter's name, although nobody dared to use it, was Four Souls from then on.

She was the making of Red Cradle, the making of her son, she was the bad wife of Shaawano, the woman who ran off with a Pillager. She was the mother of Fleur.

EACH OF US has an original, you see, living somewhere underneath the shadow of our daily life. That life we live in the moving world is the dream life of the copy. She runs, she breathes, she cares for others, she mends their clothes. You gaze into the water of your day and there your face floats back, serene, unguarded. See! See! Beneath that thin smile you are smiling somewhere else. Your hand moves and the hand moves below you. Perhaps in another country more real than you are, in another life.

Just so, the other Four Souls lived beneath the life of Fleur Pillager. Her name influenced Fleur's actions and told her what to do. How can I tell you this? How can I make you see? Sometimes it is too difficult for even an old man, one who loves to sling words. Sometimes I have trouble with this thought—how this surface of life that tosses and shatters is not the real surface. How we are dreams, blasts, shadows, insubstantial gusts of motion. That this stub of a grain dealer's pencil that moves across the page of paper is not real, either, and that the truth lies on the other side of even these words.

SIX

Figures of the Captive Graces

Polly Elizabeth

IT WAS HARD to believe that a
man who had so wonderfully stripped and profited from his holdings here on earth could so easily become that woman's dupe.
False heaven, I thought when I understood the locked door to his
room, the indiscreet sounds from within, the dazed look of foolish contentment on his face. False man, I cried aloud when not
more than a year after she had come to do the laundry the woman
was in possession of it and the entire house. In short order, sister and myself were served legally with papers. To my surprise, we
were offered a settlement so handsome that we thought it wise to
accept, particularly since Placide admitted to me that she had
practiced Karezza with her painting instructor for the whole past

year and cared little what Mauser did. Within weeks, to the astonishment of all who lived up and down the avenue, we had secured a proper house in Saint Paul and were preparing to move. And may I now say, here, that the word "Karezza" shall nevermore pass my lips? For upon the description of that discipline, innocently outlined to the doctor by my sister, Mauser was able not only to divorce Placide but to annul their marriage in the Holy Roman Church.

To the grand sobs of Mrs. Testor (who chose nonetheless to stay) and the ill-disguised happiness of Fantan, we left. Once sister and I took up life in Saint Paul, our view of the situation gained a measure of perspective and we were able to enjoy (perhaps spitefully, I admit) as well as report on the spectacle that John James soon made with his squaw.

Certainly, she had to know that people called her squaw behind her back, but never face-to-face beyond the one time Mr. Virgil Hill described. It was his sense, he thoughtfully remarked, that having addressed her as a squaw he stood in sudden danger of evisceration. It happened (he said he was quite innocent of ill intentions) as they stood by the buffet table where a huge rare roast stood pink and lucious with the carving knife temporarily abandoned by the server. He was suddenly aware how close the handle of that knife lay to the hand of the wife of John James Mauser. It was nothing he could quantify. She did not pick up the knife or even make one gesture toward it with her fingers. Yet the air between them itched.

So I shan't call Fleur "squaw" again at the safety of this remove, for I would not dare say it to her face. I do not believe in saying such things at a distance that one hasn't the boldness of nerve to say in person. I am not interested in risking *evisceration*, you can be sure. After all, my sister so completely depends upon me that I think were I to die and leave her to her own devices, she wouldn't survive the rigors of her art.

Enough to say that with me to run Placide's life she did survive. The two of us did well enough. Our portion from Mauser was such a generous maintenance that we had no complaints as far as that went. And, too, the figure that John Mauser soon presented was so pathetic, so ludicrous, that we did not feel the sting of his abandonment. People sympathized quite openly with us, though there were some men cut of a questionable fabric who professed that they understood his attraction to the Indian woman. Once she began to appear at certain functions in dramatic, daring, and yet somehow decently reserved exquisite gowns, she attracted a low sort of admiration. And then she vanished, for shame we hoped. But it turned out the reason was quite different.

Mrs. Testor became my confidante. After Fleur had ceased to appear in public, I went to visit Testor once a week, bearing a small and appropriate gift—a set of candles, a sack of licorice, a bag of scented salts—at the hour when John James Mauser and his wife were accustomed to motor out to Minnetonka to take the air or to lunch in grand style at one of the most exclusive downtown clubs. Testor fixed me a cup of tea on most days and we had a cozy little chat. On the day I learned the reason for Mrs. Mauser's concealment, I also understood that she was not at lunch but upstairs, in bed.

"She is *unwell*," said Testor, with a meaningful emphasis. I understood at once. A thick bolt of envy pierced me.

"This means an heir," I said in a neutral tone.

"So it does."

I was quiet. I tried to sip my tea, but its sweetness choked me. Having never been one to bemoan my lot, I made no expression of acknowledgment one way or the other. I don't think Mrs. Testor was of sufficient sensitivity to observe how I paled and trembled. I don't think she understood at all that sadness ran me through like a sword. I don't think she or anyone knew then, or ever will know, with what desperate eagerness I wanted a child. I took my leave, went out to the motorcar where my little dog, Diablo, sat curled on the passenger's seat. He had long since stopped begging me for anything, the little tyrant. He gazed straight ahead as though anxious to get back and eat the food in his silver bowl. So I got in, behind the wheel, and drove him home.

THE NEXT WORLD, of what shall consist its poisons and delights? Love in this world avoided me. And love's issue, beyond all measure. Immersed in the saltless broth of my existence, I tried on moods. Here was Polly Elizabeth, coy in felt slippers and hair net. Here she was parading proud in a gown of Greek influence. Now a silly *Fräulein* holding her skirts above her head. As my sister made new friends in the more advanced artistic circles of our city, she also gained a plethora of models from which to choose. And so I was left posing in cobbled-together costumes with no one to paint me. Here was Judith holding the severed head of Holofernes. Now Saint Theresa of Avila undergoing her torment by the devil. At last I could only see Polly Elizabeth, in chains of foolishness. What was I, who was I, but one considered dangerous to others from the tedium of my company?

I found myself returning with ever more frequency to the

house of my former brother-in-law. I was drawn there by the prospect of a baby, as though by a force that overpowered my will. I came to the door with a pound cake and a visiting card.

"Please bring it up to her," I said to Mrs. Testor, who regarded me with the raw shock of someone who had seen the risen dead on the day of judgment.

"Oh, shut your mouth, Nettie," I said, and stood my ground. "Can't I make it up with his new wife if I want to?"

Mrs. Testor shrugged, her eyes still round, and placed the cake and my card right next to it on the silver tray I used to carry up to Placide's studio. She brought the offering up the stairs. Came straight back down. The pound cake sat untouched. My card was turned over next to it. An eloquent rejection.

"I won't give up, Testor," I said. "I shall return. Is she craving anything? Can you give me a hint?"

Nettie Testor paused and bit her lip, struggling with some information. Where in the past I would have ordered her to tell it to me, now I mustered the patience to wait. I knew only humility on my part would unseal her lips. As I knew she would, Testor relented. She boiled a kettle of water, poured it into the brown teapot with the chipped spout, and while it steeped she told me that Fleur was having some difficulty carrying the child and there was concern she'd lose it. As Testor filled my cup, I was surprised to feel a sinking hollow in the pit of my stomach, and then a pang that made me shiver. I was suddenly anxious to return to my preciously assembled household library and consult the sections of my eugenic hygiene books that dealt with delicate pregnancies. I quickly drained my cup, thanked Testor, and told her I was going home to research the matter and find a cure.

Overexertion, overexcitement, a fall, a blow. Any violent emotion, such as anger, sudden and overpowering joy, or fright. Running, dancing, horseback riding over rough roads. Great fatigue, lifting heavy weights, purgative medicines, and, of course, excessive intercourse. Straining at the stool. Hemorrhoids. Bathing in the ocean. Nursing. Tight lacing. Footbaths are dangerous and of course shower bath is too great a shock to the system. One should avoid strenuous coughing or weeping. One should try to suppress the tendency to violent sneezing by washing the ears with tepid salt water.

There was more, much more to keeping a baby from falling out of the body before its term. I noted down every word.

Once again, the next day, I stood at the door and waited for Testor to answer and let me in. She appeared, her broad face pallid and serious. Just as she opened the door, a cry arrested her attention. Her hands flew up around her face. She whirled. I stepped in after her and when she trundled rapidly upstairs, puffing like an engine, I sprang along close behind her. She was too distracted by the cry to really notice me. She fairly charged down the corridor.

It was Fleur, of course. She had just experienced a short epoch of flooding, accompanied by sudden pains. Mauser was gone and Fantan with him, so there I was in a sudden position to take charge. I made the most of it.

"Whiskey, fetch whiskey," I ordered Testor, "and get the doctor, too."

In her panic, she obeyed by force of habit as I proceeded to gently coax Fleur to elevate her hips, the child's cradle, on some pillows. I gave her the remedy my books had recommended for the stoppage of an early derangement of the womb. Perhaps she'd never drunk the stuff before. She took a huge gulp and choked on the fire.

Slowly, slowly, I coached her, just a sip at a time and it will go down smoother.

She was furious and frightened. Her face, against the starched pillowcase that I myself had embroidered, was the color of ashes. Her eyes were black with a desperate and anthracitic heat. She gripped the pillow, as though to squeeze it dead, her hands twisting. Her voice was hoarse as she knocked back the second glass of whiskey.

"Help me!" she cried out.

And straightaway, she caught my heart.

To be needed by someone as strong as Fleur, as bold, as conscious, even though at first glance I had despised her. To be begged in a voice that God heard as well as I. To suddenly realize that if I could lay aside my small contempt, I might cherish her. I might be able to help her grow the child, the babe whom I wanted to live with a longing quite beyond my own selfish habits. By the time the whiskey had taken hold and her body quit attempting to expel the child, she had changed in my mind, but I didn't yet know how.

"CRUDE, but effective," said the doctor when he saw the whiskey. "Continue the treatment as required. Don't let her out of the bed." He called me near again as he washed his hands.

"I do not treat servants," he said, flicking water from his hands, "or Indians."

I suppose that before this moment I might have agreed with him. I might have washed his hands for him with an obsequious little smile, and handed him a clean towel to pat them dry. But at the tone of his voice, some nerve in me was strangely yanked.

"Oh? Oh? I will be certain to make her husband, *John James Mauser*, aware of your sentiments," I told the doctor, in an unmistakable rage. My voice rose. "In turn, I am sure that he will make his known to all who serve with him on the hospital board—"

But the man cut me off quite rudely by walking straight from the room without the pretense of a leave-taking. I went back into Fleur's room right away and helped her to another sip of the spirits, then sat with her, reading aloud from a book of the poems of Lord Byron, until she slept.

SO IT IS I who know as much of the truth of things as one can know. I who was privileged, who was driven to the side of a woman I'd once ordered to wash my clothes. I suppose it could be said that I was humbled, or enlarged. Some truer form of human regard had triumphed in me. The prospect of the child brought me to that. As her pregnancy continued precarious, I visited as often as I could. I worried about my distraction from Placide, but my sister barely noticed my absence and never asked my whereabouts, even when my visits grew so frequent that I spent more time in Fleur's presence than I did in my own house.

Now, to my surprise, I found it easy to be with Fleur. The room she had shared with Mauser, but now slept in alone, was very calm with its wallpaper of an eggshell brocade. The bed coverlet was made of old lace, folded down around her feet, and from that bed she watched the fire wink on the ebony mantelpiece in which were emblazoned cockleshells, the carved faces of sea nymphs, and dancing goddesses. I found it brought me peace to sit with Fleur hour upon hour. She spoke little at first and never smiled, though I think she enjoyed the music of verse. Most often, she passed her hours in a blank weariness that had in it no hint of either hostility or resentment. When my voice grew hoarse from reading aloud, I crocheted blankets for the baby or sewed pieces of a tiny layette. When my eyes failed or my fingers cramped, I simply sat and watched the afternoon light pass across the walls.

The shadows of the ash leaves as the sun moved behind them were very graceful, their movements hypnotic and sad. The radiance of late afternoon struck the fireplace and picked out the figures of the captive Graces. In that quiet, I reflected often on the house in which I'd passed my days. I had seen it raised from the beginning. I knew its natural provenance, as well as its present existence. I had watched John James Mauser build it for my sister, after all, and had been moved and impressed by the making of it.

At the time, though I had sympathized in and even acted in protest at the treatment of the horses that dragged its great blocks of stone uphill, it had not occurred to me that humans were ill treated in the matter too. All of the materials, the fabric, all the raw stuff of our opulent shelter were taken from Fleur's people. She described her natal lands and informed me of their rapine treatment at the hands of white men, at the hands of Mauser himself. As I sat in the room with the woman talking or dreaming in the bed, many thoughts came. It occurred to me to imagine her as a person—as a woman with family and feelings for them such as my own. I began to wonder who they were, and where she was from in actual truth and not the land of my misperceptions. And then, one day when she was half caught in sleep or in the whiskey the doctor prescribed and I spooned out by the hour, Fleur spoke. In a raving melancholy, she poured out language by the tub, all the time gazing straight into my eyes. Of course, I couldn't understand a single word of her vagabond tongue, but I did know she was asking for my help. That was unmistakable. She began to weep. I put my hand on her forehead and stroked her brow until she grew calmer. Piece by piece, over the weeks and months, there then grew from such moments between us a connection. And from that connection, I am not ashamed to say it, there grew love.

THE CHILD was born screaming and would not be soothed until I thought to dip my finger into the whiskey cup and lay it on his kitten's tongue. Afterward, we painted Fleur's nipples with it so that the child would suck, although, by then, as she continued her medicinal drinking, I suppose he imbibed plenty at the breast. For the first week, I slept in the cellar, in Fleur's old bed, and raced up the stairs when hearing the faintest cries. The next week, I slept on a pallet on the floor of the nursery. Soon I had the closet. Then my old room back. Nursemaid, doctor, fictional aunt, slave to the tiny one, servant to the mother too, I was in my correct element. I did all I could for Fleur, supplied the antidote for any worry, the remedy for any need, subdued any craving. I was so thoroughly immersed in my role, and in the charming new life, that only later, a good three months along, did I begin to have an inkling of what was starting to happen.

Fleur's dullness and depletion, her sunk eye, yellowed skin, had begun to give me concern. I was slightly reassured when she rallied. She took charge of herself, rose from bed, began to walk and take air. But although I could see how her strength quickly improved, I also noticed that she had acquired a taste for the stuff that had arrested her labor. She would not be without a decanter of whiskey in any room, and she sipped it throughout the day. Though I never saw her visibly intoxicated, though she never slurred her talk or stumbled, it was clear that she had began to rely on the liquor and was lost without its golden fire.

THESE WERE the happiest and the most requited times of my existence. The baby soft as butter, the blue-eyed little prince, was astonishingly like his father in coloration, and he was placid, either sweet or indifferent of temper. He started out thin and puling, but soon grew rolls and puckers, anklets and bracelets of silken fat. My continual presence at the house was accepted as long as I did not outstay my welcome, into the evening, but retired by the time John James Mauser returned for dinner. Still, I think that Mauser was amused at my enthusiasm for the boy, and perhaps sympathetic to my fervor, as it resembled his own. I found that I could sit in one place and simply stare at the baby without suffering one second of boredom or impatience. I'd never had the experience of this awed foolishness, this trance. I seemed quite brainless. I heard myself give out coos, hoots, burbles— noises I had never before uttered, animallike and almost desperate. Sometimes I gazed so long into the baby's face that I forgot my own face. Or I touched the shining hands and forgot my own borders, melted skin through skin. As I made my way home each night, I had to remind myself that he was birthed of Fleur, belonged to Mauser, that I was nothing and no relation. Yet I had given away my own heart, and once that's done there is no easy way to take it back.

SEVEN

Whiskey, Love, Linoleum

Nanapush

THE COUGHBALL of an owl is a packed lump of everything the bird can't digest—bones, fur, teeth, claws, and nails. An owl tears apart its catch, gulps it down whole, and nourishes itself on blood and flesh. The residue, the undissolvable, fuses. In the small, light, solid pellet, the frail skull of a finch, femur of a mouse, cleft necklace of vertebrae, seed-fine teeth, gray gopher and rabbit fur. A perfect compression of being. What is the essence, the soul? my Jesuit teachers used to ask of their students. What is the irreducible? I answer, what the owl pukes. That is also the story—what is left after the events in all their juices and chaos are reduced to the essence. The story—all that time does not digest.

Fleur left the reservation. Of all that happened day to day, all the ins and outs of her existence, we have what came of the accumulation. We have the story.

The coughball itself is also a valuable find. Bad omen, but good medicine. It cures headaches, too much monthly blood, fevers, flux, sore feet, love. Fleur never used it, she never needed any medicine to snag her men. They fell her way like notched trees. She treated them that way, too, and burned them with her heat or used them for her purpose. Which is how, the second time Fleur Pillager went off the reservation, she toppled Minneapolis society and made a son. But her power got to be too much for her. She got careless. Too bold. She should have known that it is wrong to bear a child for any reason but to surrender your body to life.

Fleur was what you might call stingy with her spirit gifts, and so she didn't get much back from other humans. Revenge, she wanted that. And also restoration. Don't forget. She wanted her land back and if she couldn't have the trees she wanted some equivalent justice for their loss. She was so concentrated on her plan that she could not receive. Not much love, is what I'm saying. She wasn't loved. Eyah! Of course there was Eli, but there I rest my case. Yes, she was *passioned*. Men made brainless fools out of themselves in pursuit. They adored her and feared her in equal measure, as Eli did, and as Mauser did now.

We are all imperfect in our love for one another. That is why we turn to that kind spirit who created us. Gizhe Manito tries to protect us but sometimes fails, like any parent. Yet this spirit does not stop loving us. That is the one to whom Fleur turned, I am sure of it, to argue against like a parent when everything was taken. Everything, of course, except her young daughter, Lulu.

No, she did not give her first child away. It was not as they insist. Fleur merely took the girl off to hide her the way a wolf hides a pup when she must do battle to protect her standing or confront a danger. That's how it was. Lulu was to be hidden in the government school, safe. Not left, not forgotten. This is what she did.

SHE HAD COME to kill and humiliate and take back her land, which he had stolen so carelessly that he wasn't aware of it, but then Mauser made himself her dog anyway and wanted her in such an absence of self that she put aside her knife. Whatever tenderness Fleur owned at the time was attached to her child. What love she felt was buried underneath a tree marked by a red flag. Her love was bones, or bound up in loss. No man had truly felt it. So when Mauser bared his heart and throat he knew, perhaps, the wolf in her couldn't kill him on instinct and the woman in her could not destroy him out of sheer intrigue.

He would have broken into a drenching, clear sweat, but ever since Fleur had returned his body to him, he had exercised increasing control over all of its jerks and spasms and eccentric twitches. She had healed him in order to wreck him in good condition, which to her was the only honorable way a Pillager could take satisfaction in vengeance. But healing a man is dangerous. I was going to say *a man like Mauser*. But perhaps it is dangerous for a woman to heal any man at all.

He desired her and she grew accustomed to her power. Maybe she desired him, though she would never admit it to me. Some women like a smart man, and others prefer a fool. Speaking as both, I can tell you it doesn't matter if you can convince a woman you have something to hide.

So perhaps that was how John James Mauser did it. He threw

out a net of questions, uncertainties, riddles, and Fleur dove into it, curious as an otter. She was snagged. She would be dragged along the bottom. She would be weakened and changed. His desire would exhaust her, and the high life temporarily fascinate her with its rich swirl of hilarious chimookomaanag doings and foods. She would be dazzled more than anything by the mounds of smoked white sturgeon at the party given in her honor at their wedding. For many years afterward, she talked of it. Platters of that most exquisite fish, dishes large as wagon wheels, piled high.

Uncle, she'd say, *I wish I could eat it all again!*

She withheld herself physically from Mauser until he came up with the papers and then went through with the wedding. By zhaaginaash law, she understood that his legal wife would inherit all he owned. Once she figured out how to kill him, she'd have her land back. But she could not kill him with a knife, this time— she would have to use much more subtle means, undetectable means, if that were possible. The problem was, the closer she got to the man she'd come to destroy, the muddier grew her intentions. She kept putting off his death. He took her traveling, brought her to theaters and great halls where she heard a new and violently beautiful music. They went to places where a thousand pictures were stored on the walls. He fed her the flesh of animals she'd never tasted. The meat of fruits she'd never seen. He seemed to get a hold over her in bed, too—perhaps some chimookomaan form of manaa that wrecked her resolve, at least for a short time after their marriage. That was probably when she was not careful enough with her counting of the days between moons. Anishinaabeg women had known, well before the Catholics preached it, a method of strict accounting by moon to regulate the even and timely appearance of their children. She never said it, but I believe that Mauser overwhelmed Fleur's feminine defenses, perhaps with liquor. I don't know when she first touched it, but it stands to reason that the taste of whiskey could have messed up her system of counting. For I don't believe Fleur ever meant to have a child with Mauser.

Once she carried the child, Fleur was caught and she knew it, for although she was enduring, strong, bold, and remarkable, she had a weakness. She had survived the sicknesses that destroyed the rest of the Pillagers, but she was affected by the ravage of those fevers. I only know what I've heard from listening in on the women, from things Margaret has revealed to me of women's private business. But from eavesdropping on them I understand that bearing children was dangerous for Fleur. In order not to let the child out too soon, Fleur had to stay still, keep to her bed. And that was where the whiskey got hold of her. As it has with so many of us, even myself, the liquor sneaked up and grabbed her, got into her mind and talked to her, fooled her into thinking she was thinking for herself when really it was the whiskey thinking whiskey thoughts.

IN THE YEARS after Fleur left, I had fallen into a state of keen and busy sorrow. I diverted myself with politics, stood for the tribal chairman, and immersed myself in a snow of white paper. I had argued about existence and the intentions of the whiteman's God on earth with the Jesuits and then with Father Damien, but I had never come to grips with the worst scourge ever loaded on us. Smallpox ravaged us quick, tuberculosis killed us slow, liquor made us stupid, religion meddled with our souls, but the bureaucrats did the worst and finally bored us to death. I soon found that the stacks of rules and regulations that I had to understand in order to run the tribe pinched my brain and made me even touchier than Margaret.

Along with rules, there came another affliction. Acquisition, the priest called it. Greed. There was no word in our language to describe this urge to own things we didn't need. Where before we always had a reason for each object we kept, now the sole reason was *wanting* it. People traded away their land for pianos they couldn't play and bought clothing too fancy for their own everyday use. They bought spoons made of silver when there wasn't food, and gilded picture frames when they had neither pictures nor walls. A strange frenzy for zhaaginaash stuff came over the best of us. Where before we gave our things away and were admired for our generosity, now we grew stingy and admired ourselves for what we grabbed and held. Even Margaret, whose eyes were sharp for foolishness, was overcome.

It was the nuns who changed Margaret, those women with the poor mouth souls. Ever since Margaret had visited the nuns' residence, she had wanted a floor covering like theirs. The substance they walked on was both soft and hard, she told me, and could be mopped shiny clean. It was far more beautiful than stone, earth, or wood; it was more green than leaves, with drops of cream and ink curled through it. "As though a child were playing in paint with a matchstick," she said. I nodded. I knew all about paint, for Margaret had bought paint one day and done something very beautiful and strange.

We had cleared a path to the cabin and then widened it enough to accommodate a wagon. I thought it was fine as it was, but Margaret wanted to improve this path. Somewhere, she got an idea to use the asiniig, our grandfathers, stones I had gathered in a heap near my sweat lodge just out back of the cabin. One by one, she lugged them out and placed them on either side of the road, leaving a tiny pinch of tobacco next to each one as an apology—or a request, for she had further plans. Early the next day she left for town and came back with the paint. Pink paint. With careful strokes of a brush that she made herself, from a squirrel's tail, she painted every one of those rocks leading up to our place. Pink was the color. A bright candy pink.

"Onizhishin," I said. For sure, they looked marvelous, so bright in the green scruff and dead leaves. "You've dressed up our ancestors."

"It was nothing." Margaret was modest, but I suppose my admiration for her work had some effect, for she began to improve the rest of our dwelling.

"If we have to stay in one place," she reasoned, "if we can't move around anymore and follow the rice and maple sugar and meat, then I plan to live in a good way. First, we have to make a better outhouse, just like Father Damien has drawn for us, and then . . . well, I've got an idea."

No more sitting in the sun, dreaming and smoking my pipe. Now, if I wanted Margaret to cook for me or even to give me a kind word now and then, I was forced to work. I dug a hole for trash, burned it, and scattered the ashes. I chopped and even stacked firewood. I swept clean the ground leading up to our door. Inside our cabin, we had already packed the earth down hard and laid skins over it. I took out the skins each morning and shook them clean. Instead of walking right inside we took our makizinan off at our door. We sat on the skins and blankets, or the spindly wooden chair Margaret had traded for an old buffalo hide. She had me tack up a shelf on one side of the room. There was enough pink paint to brighten the boards. The centerpiece of our cabin was a stove with a pipe running into the wall. The stove was black iron, fancy, with a small nickel grill and a cooking box. We even nailed together a small table. It now looked to me like we had a comfortable and even fancy place, and I said so, but Margaret couldn't get the nuns' floor out of her mind. She kept pining over it, stabbing her finger at the skins on our dirt floor and frowning. She kept thinking of ways to get that substance—linoleum.

I hoped that, as with many of her enthusiasms, she'd get over it. She'd once had a frenzy for making maple sugar candy in carved wooden molds. She'd gotten past that. And then there was the time she planted a garden, not with the old varieties of squash and corn, but new and outlandish seeds that produced round globes of bitter melons that blackened at the first frost, hard yellow roots to cook and mash, and tart, ripe, red love apples that stung the mouth. I thought linoleum would fade just as these other fancies had, but then I noticed that Margaret had grown distant. Her gaze had a faraway quality, as if she were peering into the future. She figured and she plotted. She found a salesman and purchased small linoleum pieces that she laid on the ground and looked at for hours, as though she could grow them across the floor by the intensity of her stare. But the bits glowed against the earth or clean skins and did nothing.

"They are dead. They never had any life," I told her. "Forget them and nestle in my arms."

Margaret waved a hand to shut me up and took out her little pipe and tobacco pouch. She loaded it, puffed away as if her brain were on fire and her thoughts were the smoke, rising in thick circles. Her eyes narrowed and she glared in a fixed black way at nothing. From time to time she gestured and nodded and smiled to some invisible person. I should have worried about her right then, but instead I grew annoyed.

"The earth is much better than the linoleum you crave, and so are the skins beneath our feet. Leave off thinking of the nuns' floor or you will sicken yourself, and me!"

But she did not, the smooth stuff gripped her. It drove her to distraction and the urge to finally acquire it ended up fracturing her will.

WE WERE snared in laws by then. Pitfalls and loopholes. Attempting to keep what was left of our land was like walking through a landscape of webs. With a flare of ink down in the capital city, rights were taken and given. Finding an answer from a local official was more difficult than tracking a single buffalo through the mazed tracks of creatures around a drinking hole. We acquired an Allotment Agent to make it easier for us to sell our land to white people. Then we got a Farmer in Charge to help us choρ our trees down, our shelter, and cut the earth up, our mother. Land dwindled until there wasn't enough to call a hunting territory. That was because we were supposed to learn to farm in the chimookomaan way, using toothed machines and clumsy, big horses to pull them. We were all going to have to plant seeds the way Margaret did, for the rest of our lives, and yet we'd only just grown used to the idea that we owned land—something that could not possibly belong to any human.

Just as the first of us had failed at growing or herding or plowing the fields, we were told we could sign a piece of paper and get money for the land, but that no one would take the land until we paid the money back. Mortgage, this was called. This piece of banker's cleverness sounded good to many. I spoke against this trick, but who listened to old Nanapush? People signed the paper, got money. Some farmed. Others came home night after night for months full of whiskey and food. Suddenly the foreclosure notice was handed out and the land was barred. It belonged to someone else. Now it appeared that our people would turn into a wandering bunch, begging at the back doors of white houses and town buildings. Then laws were passed to outlaw begging and even that was solved. No laws were passed to forbid starvation, though, and so the Anishinaabeg were free to do just that.

Yes, we were becoming a solved problem. That's what I'm saying. Who worries about the dead? They are safe in the ground.

NECTOR OWNED land that was allotted to him as a child, though he wasn't old enough to take care of it yet. Nector's land was half slough, but that's not bad, that's where the ducks land. Part field if you wanted field, or clearing, and part dense birch woods with burnt-over patches where raspberries and blueberries and tart high-bush cranberries sprouted. This land was waiting for Nector, but then one day as I was making my way back to our cabin from town, where I had traded for a jar of maple syrup, I saw that a motorized wagon as well as an ox-drawn wagon and three chimookomaanag were making a road on Nector's land. I stopped. They were chopping birch down and loading them. Clearing another field just past that.

I walked up to one of them, a brown-haired chimookomaan who gave the orders, and I said to him, "What are you doing?"

"What's it look like, old savage? Get the hell outta here or I'll fix your ugly face."

He turned away and his young muscled back covered with a moss brown shirt was like a mute wall. How this one set of humans came to be so often afflicted with a common blindness strains my powers. It's a sad thing. I quietly turned away and as I meekly disappeared around the side of their truck I added, to the gas in their tank, the maple syrup that I was bringing home for Margaret. I hated to waste good syrup, but the young pup had given me no choice.

I went home intending to speak immediately to Margaret about the matter. Her round ojiid greeted me, for she was crouched on her hands and knees when I came in. She was laying a stick marked with red lines around the bottom logs of the cabin, muttering to herself. After a while I figured out that she was measuring the floor.

"What are you doing?" I said for the second time that afternoon. And just like the thick, muscled young man clearing Nector's land, she turned her back on me. She wouldn't talk to me. After a time I understood it wasn't that she was angry, just that she was absorbed in some female dealing of her own. I watched her place the stick just so and mutter to herself until I got bored, and then I gave up and left her. Later, I regretted it, for I had to find out what Margaret had done from Bernadette Morrissey.

"SOLD IT," said Bernadette with the agent's desk between us. "Or at least part. The eighty acres that adjoins hers, she kept."

I had to make Bernadette repeat what she'd told me in Ojibwemowin in order to make certain I had the sense of it. And then, once I was satisfied that the horse-face spoke the truth, once I had looked upon the papers for myself, I was afflicted by a sorrowful anger. My sweetheart, my porcupine woman, my prickly dove, had exchanged the real ground for the false ground. My Margaret had betrayed us. She had bought her linoleum and given away Nector's earth.

NOW MARGARET had stood up with the Pillagers, and she had fought for the land. She had ignored the threats of Agent Tatro. She had fought against Agent Tatro, against the Lazarres and Morrisseys, and she had enjoyed every battle. Through the worst of things, she came out urging defiance. When her head was shaved, she'd got more vigorous instead of hiding away in shame. Her rage increased in the cold wind around her ears. The coalhod bonnet I bought for her inspired her fierce tirades and gave her confidence to rail against the agent with gall and fire. True, she had diverted the money meant to pay off the Pillager fees and applied it on Kashpaw land—but it was done in defense at least of keeping some share of the earth. Margaret was always for the land, if nothing else. Nothing stopped her in this quest, until that linoleum. Because of it, she betrayed herself, and worse, she betrayed her son.

SO WHEN I came home days after I'd found out about the sale, and when I saw that she had fit this new covering onto the floor, I did not speak. I didn't trust myself. So much given for so little. A false and foolish thing. Margaret's eye challenged me to take issue and have my say. But I did not. She knew that I knew the truth, but I said nothing, which mystified her at first. I merely shook out the newspaper that I'd picked up in town and sat down on my little bench beside the door. All that afternoon, I sat there refusing to work, an old man in the sun, while Margaret put the finishing touches on her floor. After it was glued to boards placed on the earth, smoothed, and waxed, she spent a very long time enraptured by it, moving the chair to one side, then the other, then back and forth, making a racket I knew was calculated to upset me and stir my annoyance until I boiled over and relieved her. I did not let that happen. For in truth I was afflicted with something I can't describe—perhaps a human embarrassment. Finally, she came outside and sat down beside me, eager for me to let fly at her in rage. Still, I didn't. She tried to goad me.

"How do you like the new floor?" She gave a sweet, punishing emphasis to each of the words.

I would not be trapped so easily. I nodded and said nothing. Even when she asked me so many times that it grew insulting, I could not respond. As the day dwindled, the sun from the west intensified beneath low clouds and picked out the undersides of all the leaves in gold. Margaret asked me again and again. I remained silent. Finally she quit talking and sat next to me as the light darkened in the trees.

The blue came out of the bushes. The black came out of the earth. The night was windless, moonless. I wanted to forgive her. Several times I tried to speak. But I never found the words.

EIGHT

His Comeuppance

Polly Elizabeth

*T*HE BOY refused to wean him-
self and wouldn't be coaxed onto a bottle or even a cup. He stumbled to his mother and threw himself into her lap. Even yanked
at the buttons of her shirt and bawled in fury until she gave in
and allowed him to suck. She indulged him, I thought, a bit too
long for decency, but that could hardly be helped as he was so
adamant. He yelled when she refused him. His roar was of a bull-
ish intensity that filled the house with growling echoes. But when
allowed the breast, he closed his eyes, clung to her with sweet
trust, and was the picture of such relieved desperation that I
could not imagine refusing him myself.

When he was satisfied and when he was rapt in his play, I

don't believe there ever was a prettier or more loving child. Oh, he didn't like to speak, but why should he? Every need of his was anticipated and then met before it even formed in his mind. He walked and ran and even pulled himself up the stairs at a precocious number of months. His teeth came in and shone like pearls. His hair grew long, we clipped it, then it grew in thicker yet and in summer turned a surprising pale flax color. He wore skirts and gowns. It hurt us when we had to put him in boy pants at the insistence of his father. To watch Fleur dote upon him warmed me. She was sad as I was at each sign of babyhood put away, and if he didn't speak at two years it concerned us less than it concerned his father. Fleur and I and the boy understood one another to such perfection that words were utterly unnecessary. We could play for hours in the wide sun-filled nursery and in the zoo and parks. That was true happiness. The boy brought it out of us.

During this time, Fleur made a number of day trips that, I was given to understand, had to do with a daughter by a former liaison. The girl now resided in a boarding school, and Fleur was intent on getting her to live with us. Each time Fleur left, I awaited her return with excitement, and told the boy he'd best prepare to have an older sister. But each time the driver pulled the dusty car around the curve of the drive, Fleur sat alone in the backseat. There was no child. She never let me know the entire reason she returned alone, but I understood in time that it had something to do with the girl's wishes, her pride. And so it was, the boy alone reigned over our little kingdom, and although we tried not to spoil him, it was obvious at last that we had done so. He was a commanding little thing and could get the better of us with a gesture.

One day, as Fleur was tumbling back and forth on the figured carpet of the nursery, laughing with her boy, John James Mauser entered the room. He stood watching the two at their wild play, his face rapt and charmed. Fleur was reserved around him, held herself stiffly and never smiled. It was a mystery to me why Mauser had chosen to marry her, for I'd never seen her give to him one signal of affection. He did not seem to miss it, somehow, but took his pleasure in watching her at times like these—when she was unguarded, unaware that he was watching, entirely natural. She was playful, then. I knew that side of her well. We even shared it. A love of foolishness perhaps only possible with an innocent child.

"Don't stop," said Mauser, putting up his hand when Fleur noticed him and froze. It was remarkable how she could suddenly become another person in his presence. She wasn't cold, exactly, nor did she seem angry or filled with some hidden and resenting energy. She was simply solemn and watchful. She was decorous. Within that room, she raised herself and gave the boy over into my arms. When she walked to Mauser it was with an upright gliding grace that the most polished women in Minneapolis society might envy. She took his arm. A talented mimic, she had quickly perfected her carriage, manners, behavior, by steady observation of other women.

"We must go now," she said, and as she swept past him, taking his arm, I saw that hot glow in his eyes. It was always there. He burned in the grip of some blandishment. She must know spells, I always thought, for to elicit such devotion one would think she might make some tender movement toward him. Show him some slight mark of love. He had apparently accepted his fate, though, to love unrequited and with a simple, fateless, heat. Whatever spell she laid on him, I wish I knew its verse. Can there be anything quite so remarkable and pure as devotion without recompense, devotion for devotion's art?

He folded her arm against his breast and they went out, who knows where, to some dinner, and I was left with the boy. I remember that day, it sticks. I cannot forget it. That is because it was the first day I saw something wrong with the child.

John James Mauser II had of course been to doctors, but all had pronounced him normal and even advanced, a credit to a father who sat on the hospital board. It occurs to me now that the doctors may have had suspicions, but that they had perhaps been afraid to speak frankly to one who possessed so much power over them individually and over the institution as a whole. Mauser was the hospital's primary philanthropic benefactor. Who'd dare tell such a man that his child was damaged, unwhole, fractured in mind? I myself couldn't do it, and even now I hasten to add that the boy was swift in certain other ways. Alert, he was alert in spirit I know that, though with a stranger he was apt to shut his eyes and become dull and heavy as a stone. I'd always made excuses. I saw what I wanted, doted on it, and disregarded any sign that did not fit.

But on that day, as we played sweetly together on the lion-shaped rug that his mother had bought, he suddenly went absent. He crouched beside me, very still, staring out the window into the empty sky. His blue eyes were just as vacant. He did not see me. He saw nothing, but could not be moved. For one hour, he sat there, me beside him, ever more frantically trying to coax his attention away from the nothingness where he had flown. But he was unswerving. His mouth fell open. His features coarsened into caricature. He was the very picture of idiocy. I cried out, swept him close to me, and then he began to babble. Those sounds, those syllables, those pathetic attempts. They were frightful, then, never mind the hideous they would become.

SWIFT in other ways. I said, didn't I, that young Mauser who succeeded in breaking my heart on that calm day (where others more adept had failed) was swift in other ways? Well, so he was. The boy could count. By some strange and secret method he assigned to his little world numbers, numerical values, mathematical identities. I think it started with the card playing that Fleur taught him. For he picked it up and soon it was evident that he could make lightning calculations somewhere in his puzzle box of a brain. They played cards—all in all, it was the strangest sight I ever saw. She began by teaching him little simple games, harmless child's games, but progressed until they immersed themselves daily in those matches, of which I know little, that occupy coarse men at coarse tables and are carried on under clouds of cigar smoke to the tune of clinking shot glasses. I may be too much a creature of social fears, or at any rate of rules and breeding, but I did think it wasn't right for Fleur to teach the boy every kind of poker and gambler's trick when he couldn't yet recite the alphabet.

And yet she loved him to her heart's end, yes, that could be seen. She did not believe the doctors Mauser took him to weekly, who pronounced the boy a hopeless idiot and cast his father into a depth. She remained as she was with him, cheerful and laughing. She drank her whiskey, but now more secretly I think. The only difference in their play was that mutual and growing passion for cards. John James Mauser, meanwhile, changed. Not that

Fleur would have cared to note it. But he did change, he grew still more thoughtful, and where he had always made an outward show of the Roman Catholic faith, a hypocritical nod to the church when it suited his purpose, he now became a true believer. I alone saw this occur in him. No one else thought it remarkable he went to Mass every morning before his coffee was poured. No one else was aware he took daily Eucharist and made a score of confessions every month. I suppose, being who he was, he had a lot to confess. I wonder if he ever got to the bottom of the barrel of his sins?

As he was somewhat more approachable now, and as I had by sheer ubiquity become an accepted person—perhaps an accepted annoyance to Mauser, but nonetheless accepted—I thought to ask him about his fervent adoption of religious practice. To my surprise, he took me seriously, and answered. Perhaps I should have known it was the boy's affliction that had prompted him.

"You were always aware, I think"—he regarded me with a sharp gaze—"of how I wanted a son. It was a dear wish of mine—it still is," he amended quietly. "I feel that I am responsible for this one's lack of . . ." He struggled. ". . . his abnormalities . . . his strangeness. I have come to believe that the boy's backward traits are a judgment on the man I was."

This amazing statement was forced out with honesty through pride. For the first time ever, I felt some human quality, a streak of humility, a signal of Mauser's inner workings and life, that pulled at me. Mauser had avoided me ever since his illness, hating that I'd seen him weak and outside himself in the throes of appalling fits. Now, he seemed to have put aside that old shame. He allowed himself to speak with an exhaustive frankness. Apparently, having had the time to page back through his life, he found evidence all along of the workings of a certain presence.

"An inhuman presence," he told me carefully. "I hesitate to assign God the tedious task of looking after me, but I've come to believe that I've been spared death many times in narrow circumstances by something, for something. For some reason."

I sat alertly. "I would like to hear it."

"Perhaps it is not for me to understand. If so, may it remain shrouded. But I have been spared, or rescued, or brought back to life, many times. When I was a boy, for instance, I fell through the ice of a deep pond and was known to have been submerged for nearly half an hour before I was dragged out. I came to. I survived that and I was only four years old. When I was a young hooligan I jumped a train but judged wrong and fell beneath it, managed to roll out between the wheels. Don't know how I did it. Unscathed. And then in my lumbering days a Swede dropped a pine on me. Sure, it should have killed me. But two jagged branches that might have run me through pinned me beneath the trunk, supporting it so that I was merely tapped down a little into the soft duff. I fell off a scaffold once and was caught by the belt and hung there, sixty feet off the ground. I married Placide and on our wedding day the horses spooked and ran straight over me, you remember. Not one hoof mark. Stood and brushed myself off. There was the bullet Fantan took for me in the can of sardines."

"What?" I said.

"A long story for another time." He waved that off. "And then there was my long illness after I'd so ridiculously gone to war. I did some terrible things in my younger days and was always surprised and suspicious that luck seemed to reward rather than punish me. But now I think perhaps luck was just saving for my comeuppance. Or that the just desserts that skipped over me were visited upon my son."

There she is, I thought the next day, watching from a nursery window as Fleur emerged from the car below. *His comeuppance.* It startled me to think like that, but the fact is, Mauser's history had made me shiver. It rang true. I have stopped believing in a divine lookout, but Mauser's luck was striking, or had been, until the grotesque collapse of his illness. And when Fleur cured him, I wondered now, was that a piece of good fortune or was it the beginning of a subterranean justice that now started, one catastrophe and then the next, to bring him down?

His investments began to fail. A lead mine collapsed. Securities he'd thought invulnerable to the world's flux proved otherwise. A fertilizer plant he'd owned closed and he had to sell off those lands he'd acquired by means underhanded, anyway. He was unnerved, I could see it, uncertain. Even after he came home at night, he closeted himself for hours with his accountant. When he emerged he wore a desperate, foraging look. Still, an edifice of money built as large as Mauser's, one that withstood all the world's undoing, doesn't go all at once. The daily features of life seemed changeless. The household still functioned with its usual extravagance and Mrs. Testor continued her profitable ways with the meats. Fleur's account at the dress shop was paid and the couple still appeared at social events. With her hair piled high, she still displayed the bold profile and predatory grace of a swooping bird. Mauser, although he cut as fine a figure, wore an increasingly haunted look, though maybe *hunted* is the better word.

*   *   *

MY LOVE for the boy, and the fact that I'd succeeded in drawing Mauser out on the subject of his religious habits, broke some ice between the two of us. Still, the old animosity I'd felt for his lurking manservant persisted until one day I asked about a detail of conversation that remained odd to me—Mauser's mention of the can of sardines and the bullet. I then was told the story of the way the two men forged their bond.

We sat together in the breakfast room, in pale light, our coffee on delicate gold-rimmed saucers. I wondered if he might sell them to me when the house went, then quashed my greedy thought. Mauser lighted a small cheroot and began to speak.

"My war starts with a can of sardines, a small can, unworthy of mayhem. I see it sitting in the dim illumination, there on the low table, its wrapper a bright yellow, cheerful, centering the group of men."

He tapped the cigar. I let him go on, didn't stop as he waxed thoughtful.

MOLES, human gophers, that's what we were. Burrowing creatures. I loved the dirt, craved the solid gray promise of it, nosed into the cold black safety, set my shoulders into the swing of the pick, the shovel, or dug with my face when the shelling commenced. Fantan too, here, he can tell you we loved dirt. I don't care if it was wet or dry or stank of human rot. Life in the trenches fostered adoration of the muck and the shit of survival. Don't make a face! Queen Polly Elizabeth! I swear you're a Brit, a throwback, you and your conflagrate them flower beds laid out in rows.

I first got over there. I thought to myself, why, these British, they're *short*! They were lean as weasels, too, my God, sunk in the chest and small. I thought they picked out the little ones to live in these dugouts, or maybe they were stunted by island living somehow. Come to find out, it wasn't any of my theories that held the reason I stood a head at least over even the tallest Englishman. Quite simply, the tallest had been slaughtered first. The British Recruiting Office had been forced to lower their requirements from five foot eight, I believe it was when the war began, to five foot three by the time Lloyd George started the conscription. So there I was, and Fantan, easy targets and easy picking.

"If this goes on," I said to him one foul afternoon, "think about the future of the English as a breed. The French too, I suspect. Darwin would say it is survival of the measliest. Maybe all of Europe, if it isn't one big crater, will be composed of miniature, clever, tunneling folk. Of course, there are the women, the fair and stalwart mothers and widows, as the newspapers call them back home. They'll tower. They'll lambaste and dominate. They'll thrive. They've not been culled for height or for intelligence yet. They are the ones who will run things."

Fantan concurred, agreeable then as he is now, although of course very different, my dear. I say you're British with your flowers because once I got there, moved into the trenches you see, and began to understand what a drunk fool I'd been to recruit myself, the other item that astonished me about the British was their stubborn passion for the civilized bloom. Our first shelter, which we tried absurdly to make comfortable, was actually decorated all around the door with the trained vine of a climbing sweet pea. The girlfriend of some poor poetic cluck had sent the seeds on his request. He was blown to literal pieces before the show of the first bud, so it was left for the rest of us to enjoy the bower. The damn blossoms were enormous, hot pink, lavender, and white, fertilized by human guts.

Oh, you've gone pale green, Polly Elizabeth. Your mother wouldn't have sat still this long. But you feel sorry for me, don't you, or is it something else? I know you're sick to the gills of Fantan, of putting up with him. You want to know why I brought him back, of course, and why I won't let you, any more than I permitted your mother, toss him to the church or the veterans' ward. You want to know how I won him, or he won me, or we became possessed of each other. Since you can't ask him, you're asking me. I'll answer, too, it's easy. A can of sardines.

All right, then, another coffee, that will do.

The sardines had got to be a kind of joke in the lulls. There were these times when not much went on beyond the pounding of guns, the sniping, and the occasional man hit north or south of you. There were evenings we sat in the dugout, which we'd banked well and scratched deeper and deeper into the earth and improved, even with a scrap of rug, a crate, a table of sorts, so that we thought our burrow was pretty grand—spacious and well concealed and snug. There were these two men, a couple, mates they called themselves, like Fantan and me. Bert Chiswick and Mr. Dragon were their names. The two thought themselves mighty clever when it came to bridge, which I despise. But we played it with them, had to before they would put themselves out for whist, pinochle, or especially poker, which from his name you might infer my friend Fantan knew a great deal more than a little something.

As a matter of fact, it was how he had made his living in New Orleans, and the reason he joined up with me, the both of us in ardent flight, he from an unsustainable loss, welshing out of a debt, and I from your sister, who had me so far in the hole I didn't know how I'd get out with her, either. I'm not going to dwell on that, however, don't purse your lips. Fantan had possession of the can of sardines, something we'd kept circulating there among us, one winning it, then the other, though most times it sat in Fantan's breast pocket, guarded against theft. There wasn't much else that we could play for, you see, and the can had a rather nice heft to it by then, a history like the sweet pea vine, a familiarity and weight, like a talisman once you carried it. And indeed, no one had been hit while in possession of the can, that much was true. I can still see it—the worn yellow seal, the fading print. PRINCE OF WALES BRISLINGS IN MUSTARD SAUCE, the small black official-looking seal down in the corner. FISHMONGERS TO THE KING had been torn or rubbed away, but the aura clung. I associated the can with the royals in each suit and imagined the King himself, flapping his linen serviette from its folds, sitting down to a steaming cup of brewed tea one morning, his servant lifting the silver dome away from a Wedgwood plate that held rounds of sweet buttered toast, an egg, poached of course, and one perfect Prince of Wales Brisling with a dollop of its own fishy mustard sauce athwart the tail.

Fantan made his living by his wits and by his looks too, I should add. Women clung to his boots, though I suppose you're immune to such things, schooled by the redoubtable Hammond of the Ham Bosoms, a polish on you, porcelain finish that wipes clean, resistant to finger marks or any foul smears a man might leave there. But I've gone astray again, haven't I, sister. I do apologize. It was on that cold afternoon, suspecting we would have to prepare for an attack, our gas equipment piled at each of our elbows, that we dealt for the can.

I was its most recent host, but after the game Fantan was the new possessor. We were laughing. I removed it from my breast pocket and just as I passed it over to him the luck ran out of the can. For as I bent to scoop the cards up as well, the can blew straight out of my fingers. Blasted forward by a sniper's bullet, the can exploded up through Fantan's chin, slicing his tongue and thereby correcting his speech forever of his frequent obscenities and much else too. That was the beginning of a fierce attack that shot my lungs and scored my nerves—I was no good after seeing Fantan's mouth shredded by the can. No good after seeing so many other things, Polly Elizabeth, that made his poor wound as nothing. No good, no good, and after raving for some months sent back here. Insisted that Fantan stay with me, forever. Now you know why.

I WAS QUIET. I had put down my coffee. Fantan had come into the room and now we looked at each other steadily. I noticed his brown eyes, the lashes darkened as if by soot. I had never seen him as a man or even known he was intelligent. He wouldn't speak to me because he knew I despised him and he even affected foolish maneuvers around me, which I now saw were ploys. The two had laughed behind my back at my dismissal, at my prudery, and my sorry treatment of the man was suddenly a feature of livid shame. I believe I went red and caught my breath in and wished to cry.

"No, no," said Mauser, dropping his hand on mine. His hard brown hand. "Fantan doesn't hold it against you, now, do you, Fantan?" Through tears, I gazed up at the savior of the father of the boy I thought of, a fancy of mine, as my godchild. Fantan looked down at me with some amusement. He shrugged to show that my approval or disdain was all the same to him, and I began to laugh. So you see, once a person drops the scales of prejudiced certainty and doubts appear, there is no telling how far a heart can open. Even toward Fantan. From outside, there was Mr. Mauser and his rare creature of a wife, his heir, his proud household. A solid construction. Scandalous, perhaps, but wealth fixes that. From within, I saw a poor collection of wrecked knaves and flawed hearts, and where before I'd had to mask such truths, now the honest understanding provided comfort. We had our shortcomings, at least, in common, if not our triumphs.

NINE

Love Snare

Nanapush

A MAN FINDS happiness so
fleetingly, like the petals melting off a prairie rose. Even as you
touch that feeling it dries up, leaving only the dust of that emotion, a powder of hope. That is how it happened with me. There
was more to these years than what happened to Fleur, of course,
in her faraway mansion in the city. Out of Margaret's linoleum
there developed a life-and-death struggle of my own, right here on
the reservation. No sooner had Margaret Kashpaw installed her
new floor, and no sooner had I taken a dizzy swallow of air and at
last forgiven her for it, than our joy was disrupted. Our peace was
shattered. Our love was challenged. My life's enemy, Shesheeb,
returned to set up his house down my road. He lived yet, though
I'd tried to kill him many times.

Nothing is complete without its shadow. Shesheeb was the older half brother of Pauline Puyat, who'd left to pray herself into a lean old vulture. Perhaps Shesheeb came to take her place on the reservation—otherwise I suppose we would have been too light, too sun-filled, too trusting, and floated up without our anchors of dark.

Ever since he was born and guns sounded across the lake, Shesheeb had been my special foe. My mother said that when I heard those guns crack I cried and went stiff with rage in her arms. Even when we were babies, I believe he lay waiting to singe me in his cradle board, his tikinaagan. Or to whip me with a lash made of deerhide strips off his mother's tanning frame. For he did these things. While we were still small, he stood on the far edge of a slough in late fall, after a light dust of snow, and called me across the ice with a frantic wave and cry so that I bounded onto the thin crust, skidding with alarm, and went through. If he'd only laughed! But he just looked at me from the other side with sly, gloating wonder.

He was given to his aunt, Iron Sky, to raise. She gave him the charcoal, the burnt stick, the ashes, which was a sign for him to fast and find his vision and his spirit helpers. One morning, he darkened his face and went off into the woods to ask for help, which never came. His aunt gave him the charcoal again, and then again. Nothing. Finally he snatched it from her grip with a glare and went out to fast until he grew so gaunt his nose stuck out and his eyes were big and staring in his head. Iron Sky would not give up—she knew already that the mind of her boy was a complex knot. Only for the manidoog to untangle, she said, or to cut. The last time she sent him out he was nearly dead once he returned. He staggered and dropped flat over on the path. It was on that trip that something happened to him we can't say, we don't know, we haven't a name for and don't want one. Listen.

When he came back, he stared straight at everyone as if to capture or pierce. Only, if you looked back, as I dared to do, his eyes flickered away—flat, nerveless. He needed to get near people. He would not be alone, and glanced around in a constant, anxious way to see who noticed him or as though he was followed. What did he see? Form of the owl, flight soundless, a ruffled heart. Nightseeing and invisible. Balls of crackling light. A man paced swiftly with his head twisted backward on his neck. Two rabbits screamed from the same snare. Shesheeb discovered cruelty. He cut the tongue from a slow, harmless porcupine and watched it stand in surprise there at his feet, bleeding until it toppled. He laughed, and Iron Sky understood that to laugh at the pain of a harmless animal is the sign of a mind twisting in on itself. She sent him from her place soon after, with her thoughts shut carefully on what he had become.

He took up wandering, from one house to another, always sent to the next place, until he came to us. My family took him in for a short time, to our sorrow. I remember the sap was running when he got his name. My father wore two earrings, and bending over the boiling sap one fell off into the kettle. He didn't notice until the boy who was staying with us reached in to grab it. His hand plunged down. He let out a sly and greedy quack. The noise startled us. He made the sound again, looking at his boiled hand, the earring. Quack! And so Shesheeb was named for the black duck, greasy and sly.

How he got my sister to marry him, I don't know. For he grew up to look like a duck, fat and juicy, with a potbelly and a broad, flat nose, a shovel face, gleaming feathers for hair and a bowlegged hunch. His eyes used to be small and bright, though it was said that now he was almost blind. His laugh was doubtless the same sardonic quack he used when, much younger, he had struck his young wife with a burning stick. The blow marked the side of my sister's lovely face with a knot of flesh that grew darker and darker, until it swallowed her. Then came the winter of our last starvation, when she disappeared. I know what happened. The truth is this: Shesheeb went windigo. That he killed and ate my sister was never proved in a whiteman's court, so he went free. But the rest of us knew.

Shesheeb married into the Lazarres. He dragged his second wife out onto the plains, into Bwaan country. So he was yet aligned with them, and now, he had come back to doctor them and to lead them in their opposition to all I stood for on the council, as the tribal chairman, and as myself.

Ever since the first snow, he had settled down the road in a little gray house that used to belong to Iron Sky. How he put his hands on her tiny, handsome, tidily kept place I do not know. But from there, I could sense him. He was a splinter in my foot that pierced me when I stepped down hard. A darkness that rose just beyond the edges of the woods. I could feel him out there and I could smell his charred feathers. Crippled in one foot, he limped and duckwalked through the bush gathering black medicines. Lazarres came visiting him, but they avoided Kashpaw ground. And from his front door, from wherever he could, the old dog tried to steal my Margaret.

Margaret's churchgoing piety dictated that she always beat

Father Damien to Mass, and her tendency to scold and worry always made her late in leaving me. Therefore, it was her habit to take shortcuts across the land of Shesheeb, to pass near his cabin. More than once, she had returned with a report that he'd tried to waylay her with clever talk. Maybe he needed someone to keep his old bones warm in his cold winter blankets. Or perhaps he had seen her once too often, noticed the bold secret of her look, felt the prickle of her provocative scorn.

"You stay away from him today," I warned her as she put warm wrappings on her legs and bundled on her heaviest coat.

Margaret's gaze sharpened and she smiled into her beaded drawstring bag, counting the coins she was so save-y with. Her hair had not grown back as thick after her braids were severed, and her strength was less because of it, but strands of inky black still shone even in the winter light, and Margaret still possessed the mental fever that acted on me like a love charm. She blew hot, then cold, chilled me, scorched my fingers on those rare times she welcomed my touch. Never hiding her thoughts, her words were playful as arrows.

"Shesheeb?" Margaret made her voice falsely innocent. "He talks sweet to me when I pass by, I like the things he says."

I gripped the knob of my willow stick, thrust it hard at the swirling pattern of Margaret's floor.

"Don't poke my linoleum!"

"Your linoleum, your spanking new linoleum, that's all I hear! What does the stringy old duck tell you?"

"He says I have a round cheek," she explained with some pride. "I have a young walk, my legs look plump, my thighs sweet and tender."

"He's just hungry." I dragged my stick in a deliberate scrape and banged it on the floor to anger her. "Besides, I've heard the old prick's half blind." She kicked my cane from my hands.

"The only stiff thing you own!"

Margaret puckered up her lips and left me, her walk swift and firm. Shesheeb was right about her cheek and legs and thighs, and I was wrong not to follow her that day. For maybe he got an answer, a glance from her eye that encouraged him, a pout from those lips he would probably call juicy, though toward me they were thin, set, and stern. Maybe that, or Shesheeb could have done some darker work. It could be that he hid a love packet in the snow of the path she walked—clippings of his hair and nails, the coughball of an owl, Margaret's and his own hair twisted together. Stepping over it, perhaps Margaret felt a low warmth, a hot breath along her neck, a chinook wind flowing through her arms, her blood, an early spring. I could see it! Her thoughts melted and softened, too sudden. She raised her basket and sang an old French tune.

The time she was gone to Mass lengthened and its passage seemed too slow. I tried singing. I tried chopping wood. I tried to distract myself by drumming and then by mudding the log sides of our cabin. But my mind ran over scenes of Shesheeb seducing Margaret until I was a wagon dragged by the runaway horses of my jealousy. And then, when she finally returned with the smell of incense in her clothes, I watched her with close, testing eyes. I thought that she looked too cheerful—in her cheeks wild roses flushed. *Winter chinook, for sure,* I decided in an inner fury. He'd used his love ways, his bad old powers on her, used his clever tonics and suggestions, or that black stare from under his eyebrows said to draw women to him like chaff to a knife.

That night Margaret turned her back to me as we lay wrapped in our blankets. She knocked my hand off her breast, pressed her lips shut against my kiss. I couldn't sleep, and so I was alert when in her dreams she mumbled something slow and soft that could have been his name. Shesheeb! Hearing that, I sprang up, away from her side, my throat choked with blazing poison. Again, I was young and hot-blooded, ready to grab and kill with my bare hands. Of course, he wasn't in reach and in fact I wasn't even sure I'd read Margaret's sigh correctly with my fuzzy hearing. Still, in my doubt, I was unable to settle next to her in peace and so I went out the door. The night cold was deep, the icy wind dry and sharp. I breathed desperate, cold drafts, sucking in the air. At last, a calmer, puzzled spot cracked open deep in my heart, and I remembered my sister.

IN THAT MONTH of the year when the snow is rotten and the deer starve, Shesheeb had come to court my sister. She was round as a prairie hen, with a surprised mouth, always laughing and curious. Her eyes were soft and wondering. Simple ways, she had her simple ways. Fifteen summers she had bobbed on the stalk of her family like a sweet blossom, unfolding her petals. Fifteen autumns had taught her sorrow and to work hard, to put away all she could save for the winter. Fifteen springs she had budded with tender inner life. But the year of Shesheeb would teach her more than I know, even now, when I have seen four seasons go around fifty times and more.

I was only one year older, so she and I shared a mind. Children do that when they are left alone to dream up their games. I was half grown before I knew her feelings weren't my feelings, her

105

thoughts were not my thoughts, her laugh came out of her mouth alone and not mine. Still, the closeness lingered, so that when Shesheeb came calling, slouching in to sit near her on the ground, sliding his finger up her arm, darting his eyes down the side of her throat until her cheeks went hot, I understood her fascination. Hated, but understood. The mind of my sister was beautifully wound, a fine skein, a perfect spool. Shesheeb took hold of the end of the string and then, slowly, he unraveled her.

I SHOOK my head to clear it of old sorrows. My thoughts came up out of my mind like the steam from a bear's winter den. I tried to calm myself. Perhaps I gave Shesheeb too much credit for his powers. Perhaps he was not as clever as I feared. There was no sound in the woods and it was perfectly dark. Tonight, at least, the old man traveled in no ball of light. I heard no evil calls or whistles of medicine pitched out from his direction. It occurred to me that perhaps I should look at Shesheeb's return in a different way. What if I began to view the old man from a position of strength? What if I had drawn him back to *me* in order to take vengeance? What if I triumphed? These were sudden and heady thoughts. In the black silence of the night they made my blood hot, my eye keen. I tasted fresh blood and I saw my enemy in pain, begging for his life.

I would medicine him, poison him, kill him. I knew how to do it from the old man who taught me everything—Mirage. Right then, right there, I sat down. I planned my medicines. I even mixed some from a pouch and the ground beside me, for I knew a recipe. That night, I sent the greasy old duck, Shesheeb, a dream in which his penis hopped off his body then became a cricket and was snapped up by a thrush as he lunged to save it. A dream where his rear end spoke and his lips were sealed. Where the road turned to stew and he bent to eat it and broke his few remaining precious teeth on the rocks. I went further. The blackness overcame me then. I sent a dream where I sank my teeth into his throat and ripped through his guts with claws grown as sharp as an eagle's. I laughed without mercy and crushed him with my slow weight. I tied him up and spat on him. I humbled him. I devoured him and I spat out the bones.

When morning came I made my way back into the cabin to crawl, spent from my imaginary victories, into bed beside Margaret. My mind was still crowded with ghosts. But thinking of my sister had strengthened my heart. I would not be beaten. Not again. Not this time. I would save Margaret whether she liked it or not.

THE NEXT MORNING was the Feast Day of some purse-mouthed saint or other, and to the surprise of Margaret, I was nothing but pleasant as she readied herself for Mass. Even when she put on her great black coal-hod bonnet, the one she believed gave her an irresistible allure, I only complimented her.

"It casts a mysterious shadow upon your face," I said. "It makes a man wonder just what you might do next."

"This, probably," she said, and whacked my shin with the stick she used for walking. But I could tell she was unnerved by my sudden too-affable acceptance of her flirtation. Maybe she was even disappointed. For sure, as she left the cabin, she was just a little anxious, since she may have sensed the cold truth of what my plan called for. Having taken advantage of the situation, having decided to turn things my way, I decided to use Margaret as bait.

I would ruin him before he harmed her. I would wreck him with my power. Already, he was probably sick and reeling from the dreams he'd suffered. He hadn't a hope once I started on him in earnest with my medicine. Now, before Margaret put on her old gray wool blanket coat, I took from my sack of powders and teas a packet that held the gall of a mink. A pinch of that mixed with ground mica, so his eye would be dazzled. The ashes of two dogs killed in copulation. I dusted the back of Margaret's coat, as she walked out, with the deadly attractant. I hoped that when he made a false move, and she lambasted him, she'd not only leave a mark but he would leave something with her. I needed a swatch of hair, a button, a few threads of his clothing, something he wore close to his body, in order to best him.

Now I have hardly ever had to fiddle with dark medicine, and I didn't feel that good about using Margaret. But an old man who has survived this long does so at some risk to his principles. I couldn't afford to stack myself above the problem when the stakes were the woman I loved.

I sat on my bench just outside the cabin door where I could see the crossroads and while she was gone I anxiously watched the world pass by. There went George Bizhiew with his blood palomino. There went Short Little Sweetheart. There went Mrs. Cardinal. I waited. I tried to let my mind travel after Margaret, but I think she knew it. She blocked my vision. Hung a curtain down across my sight. For I was left in a dark frustration until at last I saw the black curve of her bonnet as she returned through the scrub oak and alder that grew across the road.

She wasn't steaming forward in a heat of indignation. She wasn't in a cold and offended dudgeon. She wasn't in a fury of motion and she didn't poke at me with her stick or make a single sharp comment as she passed by me and into the house. I heard the scrape of pots, her careful arrangements as she prepared to cook. I stood behind her, examining her back for signs of Shesheeb. But there was nothing. Not one hair. Had he made a move on her? Had the bait worked? I couldn't tell, and finally gave up. She served me food. I tasted cautiously. I tasted with careful thought. And what I tasted was not the careless and bitter old porridge she'd serve to me when angry, nor was it the succulent tidbit she'd save in the lean-to for those rare times I fell into her favor.

That afternoon, Margaret cooked me a decent stew composed of a rabbit she had snared and skinned just that morning. She boiled it with an onion, a few potatoes, a can of Red Jacket Beans, and a little bacon and pepper just for seasoning. I ate the first bite with curiosity, the next with gratitude, and joy, but every spoonful after that with increasing suspicion.

This was all too much the stew of a dutiful wife, which Margaret was not. The rabbit indicated humble industry on her behalf, planning, forethought. She must have set her snare last night and risen very early to check it. For days before that, even, she must have followed and noted the trails of rabbits. The can of beans had been waiting on our shelf for an occasion. And the onion. Where had she hidden such a thing? Had she perhaps brought it home from Mass in the cup of her bonnet? Was it a prize acquired from the nuns? Or was it, and here a bleak pang of outrage choked me, could this onion be a little love gift, an offering, a sly come-hither threat from Shesheeb?

I put my spoon down. My blood was thickening in my veins. My voice went ragged with fearful speculation. I should have kept my mouth shut, but couldn't help myself.

"There is dirt in this stew," I said to Margaret.

She shook her head as though she couldn't have heard right, and then gave me a sour but still friendly look, as though my little joke had missed its mark. That was when I should have stopped. But then I tasted the potatoes. They were soft on my tongue, silken with gravy. I couldn't remember where we kept the potatoes, whether we had potatoes, if potatoes had ever been inside our house, or within my reach, or if they ever existed anywhere on earth.

"Rotten to begin with!" My voice came out a shriek. Jealousy, that spider, sank its fangs in my heart. I jumped up and began accusing Margaret of small things and, when she laughed in contempt, of large and then outrageous things I knew were far beneath her. "And if you think that this stew will quench my fire," I finished, "you are mistaken. I will definitely kill that greasy duck."

Margaret calmly rose, took the stew outside, and dumped it. "For the dogs," she said. "They deserve it more than you."

I sat down, my face to the wall, trying to contain myself. I hadn't thought that she would dump the stew, which was, after all, delicious. We so rarely had anything good to eat that her action shocked me back into my senses, as it was meant to. Only by exercising the utmost restraint did I keep myself from rushing outside with my spoon, beating off the dogs, scooping what was left into my mouth before it soaked into the earth. It took more effort yet to keep from expressing my regrets about my hasty words. To apologize to Margaret was to give her a sharper knife to cut me with, and since the whole thrust of my life was to dull her blade, I shut my mouth.

LOVE POWDERS sometimes double back and land upon their maker, which is why an expert is always required in their use. I learned what I know from the greatest of them all, Mirage, who peopled a tribe. The next day, I worked hard on a love medicine, smoked and thought over the ingredients. I had decided to put together the most potent batch I'd ever concocted, and use it. I'd lost all pride and only wanted a secure hold on my love, my Margaret, but something worked against me. Something or some person.

There was a pack of dogs that roamed the reservation, sometimes vicious, sometimes craven, and always starving. One of them was Shesheeb's dog—the skinniest and saddest of them all. The dogs had gulped the stew. Of course, finding such good pickings, they came the next day for more and hung around watching with careful eyes. I sat on the bench beside the door, my ingredients beside me. As I worked on the medicine, they drew near. I suppose that my grinding up roots and burning off the ends of hairs and wetting and singeing leaves got their juices flowing, quickened their responses, made them pant. I turned away from my work, once, went inside the house to fetch something. When I came back outside again I saw that the leanest, saddest, runtiest-looking little gray dog of them all had leaped onto the stump just before the bench where I'd put the tray of finished medicine. That dog, Shesheeb's dog, was licking up the powder.

"Awus!" I yelled and chased him off, but he'd been too quick for me. The stuff was gone. The dog had just eaten a batch of love powder stronger than any other I had ever made, and although the loss was hard I couldn't help wishing that I could tell what just happened to Margaret. She would laugh. The poorest, weakest-looking, scroungiest, ball-headed mutt of them all had had the quickness and cleverness to make his move! I wondered for a moment what would come of it, but soon forgot. I had my own pressing troubles. Margaret. I wanted Margaret. I wanted to make her eye spark. To make her turn toward me like a plant toward sun, a child to the drum. She would be mine, I decided, and started all over with the preparations for the medicine. No dog would get it this time. But I couldn't rely on medicine alone. I had to make up for the insult I'd delivered with my suspicions about the reasons for that stew. And I tried, but I think I was too close. Or perhaps I was trembling with an old man's desperation. She was my last love, and the most challenging of all my life.

We were meant to face death together, Margaret and I, for what else is love in old age? On those occasions when our animosity melted and turned golden, I brimmed with such comfort that death lost a portion of its wretched power. I am an elder. Supposedly wise. Supposedly I am resigned to, familiar with, prepared for the end of my life. But the more I know of death, the more I fight death. I am at war, angry at death's greed for the living. In fact, I've vowed to elude death as long as possible, to spite and despise death, along with Margaret. We are alike—tough, slippery, shrewd, unrepentant—though of course she showed a different face to the priest.

Perhaps my hand slipped as I ground up my powder, or my mind was distracted, and I got my proportions disarranged. For even as I was working a new medicine beneath the blade of a knife, and smoking off the ingredients with sage, I felt myself losing control. I felt the rage taking over, the poison, the sorrow over what Shesheeb had done to my sister long ago and what he was intent on doing now. A red fury seized me, heating up the marrow of my bones. I transferred the powder from the table to a twist of cloth. I had never before needed medicine to snag my women. They came to me! This humiliation was his fault, as was the anguish of my sister's death.

I put down the powder, then stashed it away.

I'd had enough of him, too much for a lifetime, I decided. Before I was forced into the shame of putting a succession of love powders on my old lady, I would go out, hunting duck. I would find Shesheeb and kill him.

Only what method should I use?

I ticked off the most effective as I walked the wood. Poisoning was good, but I'd have to gain his trust, get near him, and that I didn't think I could stomach. I wasn't much good with knives— my arms had lost their strength and my grip was weak. I could shoot him, but killing with a gun wasn't very manly and besides, it was a fast and undeservedly merciful death. I went through them all and wasn't satisfied with any one of them until I chanced to remember that I had once snared a man—Clarence Morrissey. That snare had been effective, satisfying, cheap. True, I had let the dog live, but I would have no such pity on Shesheeb.

That day, my walk took me into the trading store to buy a good long length of wire for a snare. I put the wire on credit, which both Margaret and I paid up as rarely as possible, in the hope that if we did have to die we would go with a whopping bill. I looped the wire and carried it in my shirt. On the way home, I investigated all the paths I thought Shesheeb might walk, crept close enough to his place, his den, his lair of shame so I could smell the burnt grease of his cooking. It took some time.

I didn't set my snare the first day, I didn't set it the second day either. I waited and I thought, crept back to look for tracks and ascertain his habits. I knew that I'd have only one chance. The drop beneath the snare I had used on the Morrissey was made in winter, much easier to dig out from beneath. Much easier to hide. This would be difficult. I finally settled on a slim trail near his house, a straight bit with a bend just beyond. A natural place to look up, and pause, just in case a bear or who knows what might be coming around the corner. And after looking to step ahead freely. To brush through a fringe of leaves. In those leaves, the narrowest part, I would set the wire loop. But first I dug a shallow pan into the ground—here Shesheeb's toes would dance, touch earth with a tantalizing desperation, twitch, die. My heart flinches in me now that I think of the strict care I took. How I made sure the noose slipped easily, shut lethally, squeezed, cut. How I calculated and removed all that his hands might clutch and made the hole extra wide and deeper than necessary. It was just a good thing I calculated heavy—for his potbelly and his fat head and his duck feet. Fortunate a wind dropped a light branch across my deadfall trap. Oh yes, very lucky!

FOR THREE DAYS, nothing. The sky was bleak and gray. I kept a strict watch and checked often. But maybe Shesheeb's old bones ached and he'd stayed in the house. Maybe he was making some underhanded medicine of his own, maybe he was just smart. On day four a wind stirred and blew the clouds off. Through the scraps of white the sky blazed out, welcome and blue. I sat down on the little bench I had placed beside the cabin door and let the sun hit me. The warmth baked my old bones. I smelled the calm freshness of the rain drying off the leaves. I let myself dream, as I do so often now, of the old days and old people. The women gambling beside the lake. The summer gatherings when we picked berries and made our babies. The winter fires and the aadizokaanag, the stories that branched off and looped back and continued in a narrative made to imitate the flowers on a vine. I thought of tracks, joyous, dense, when we camped along the river, and how our tracks were now scattered and few. I relaxed against the sun-soaked wood of the cabin's southern wall. I lived in my thoughts. I remembered my sister's gentle and indulgent laugh—she was never harsh—and I felt the light touch of her fingers on my hair. A sound penetrated my fog of memory, a high-pitched and prolonged squeak not unlike the death yell of a rabbit.

I jumped up, made my way into the woods. The sound wasn't human, but I didn't expect Shesheeb to die with dignity. Indeed, I'd made as certain as I could that he'd die in shame. As I ran through the woods, or at least hobbled fast as my old bones would take me, the squeal increased its penetrating intensity. The pitch grew higher, wilder, shaking me to the core, even though I've hunted all my life, and fought, and seen men die in difficult ways. It was not a man, however, whose death rang through the leaves. Rounding the corner, I looked and skidded to a halt in wild shock, for it was Margaret I'd snared.

She strained on perfect tiptoe, like a zhaaginaash ballerina dancer, on the flimsy branch that had fallen across the shallow square that I had carved in the path. Her hands were up around her neck attempting to release the tightening wire. Her face was dark red. When she saw me she went silent. For the first time, ever, I had her complete attention. Even in my horror I was somehow gratified, and of course I was on fire to save her. She looked at me with such appeal and in such a state of frantic desperation that I would have done anything, changed places with her if I could. I threw myself down, and crept forward. Terrified to lose her balance, she froze. I edged closer until I was crouched nearly underneath her. She understood my plan and stepped onto my back. Though it might break me, I intended to rise. I marshaled every bit of my strength and lifted her enough so the wire loosened and she was able to pull it over her head. Once she was free, she fell, retching and gasping, beside me in the ditch.

Now that I had saved her, now that she was assured of life, I had only a few moments in which to work on her logic. Because I had included young Nector in plotting and executing my long-ago revenge on the Morrissey, I'd never told Margaret that I was the one who'd set the snare. I positively didn't want her to connect me with the snare now. Not that I really wanted to lie. I'd tell her later, I decided, when the memory of her experience had dulled. For now, I could see no harm in assigning blame where it would work to my advantage. Therefore, as I scrambled for my walking stick, I cried out, "Shesheeb! Can't he stick to bad medicine? Must he also set snares all around his house?" Then I gasped, and wheezed, pounded the earth, and vowed I would tear into him right away, crack his skull with my diamond willow stick, beat him senseless for trying to snare my wife.

"Your wife?" said Margaret, rubbing her neck, tough-minded in spite of her near death. "Even now I am holding out for a church wedding, old man, so we'll get to that 'wife' part later. For now, quiet down. Akiwenzii, I have had a vision." Margaret dragged me to her, grasped my jacket, spoke face-to-face in an earnest and serious voice. "Bizindan. Listen to me, Nanapush."

As we walked back together, dragging ourselves home through the woods, both weak and giddy with relief, Margaret told me the substance of her revelation. Many times we had to stop, for she spoke with great force, breathing hard. What she'd seen was

116

no less than a spirit gift, a revelation that could change her life and mine, too. I didn't know whether to be horrified or proud that I had caused it, I only knew I should for once be quiet as she spoke.

"As the dark closed in around me, as I choked, as I was near death," Margaret said, "here is what happened, old man. I saw my great-grandmother from the old days. You know the one. They used to call the old lady Medicine Dress. She came to me, looking different from when she died. In my vision she was young and strong. She wore her dress, the medicine dress that she was known for. That dress was powerful. That dress was known for its healing powers. And then she told me its secret, which she'd never told a living person. That secret had died with her but she was giving it to me now, she said, in order to save my life. Here is what she told me. Nothing upon that dress was ever touched by a human, much less a chimookomaan. It was sewn for her by the spirits, she said. Then she told me I must sew my own dress, just like it. Since she couldn't get the spirits to do the whole thing, I had to follow the other rules she would set out. She said once I had made this dress, I would have great power. In this dress, I could heal anyone. I'd see things when I wore this dress. I'd know things beyond the reach of my mind. After she told this to me, blackness closed around my eyes. I could see no longer. I experienced great sorrow, believing that I would die before I could create this healing dress. I looked up into the sky, and there I saw a circle of women. I heard them dancing— their soft footsteps slapping the earth. I was pierced by the wish to live, opened my eyes, and then saw you! Old man, you have saved me to outfit this vision, to make myself the medicine dress!"

Margaret's eyes widened and then softened to a deep maple color, and her gaze stuck to me, charming me close. "Dear old man," she said softly now. "You saved my life and made it possible to sew my vision. Let me show you my thanks."

As we walked down the path toward our cabin, she clasped my hand in hers and I decided there was no reason at all for her ever, ever, to know I'd set the snare.

TEN

If She Will Have Me Now

Polly Elizabeth

I FOUND THAT I liked living by
my own laws, not Miss Hammond's, and by my own law's devis-
ing I saw at last that I should step out of place and speak to
Mauser about the state that his household had fallen into since
the birth of his son. With Testor in charge and Fleur indifferent
to overseeing expenditures, what appeared at table was but a frac-
tion of what was cooked and consumed. The monthly butcher's
bill was what one might expect for an outgoing steamship—to
stock it for a transatlantic crossing. Veal chops might appear at
dinner, perfectly cooked, but the rest of the calf from ear to split
hoof was devoured by Testor's family and by friends of the family

and by the whole neighborhood, I wouldn't be surprised. I hated to turn tattle on the woman, but after all, I had given her fair warning where my loyalties lay.

So that was how I made myself essentials again, even as the boy grew past the bounds of my care. It happened suddenly, with a bewildering rush, in fact. He seemed to enlarge by the hour, by the day. He burst from his clothes and could not fit into our laps. Sly hungers developed in him. I had to lock the cabinet where our new cook kept the sugar and all sweets, yet one night he pried into it with a butcher knife. He'd pour the contents of a sugar bowl straight down his throat. Weep wretchedly on those rare times he was denied. He began to frighten me. He was as big as some boy twice his age. Then suddenly he stopped growing upward and grew outward, became very plump. It was all we could do to contain him, and then we couldn't contain him. Where before he had run the household on the whim of his charms, now he ran it by the strange dictates of his temperament.

Some days, I woke to the sound I began to dread, a rhythmical creak. A certain floorboard gave persistently in the corner of his bedroom where he liked to rock, sitting on the floor, his fist in his mouth. He stared at nothing then. He wouldn't know me when I came in or be stopped or soothed out of his gross repetition by any means. Even Fleur couldn't pull him from his trance, not that she tried. In fact, at those times, she would sit with him. Simply sit. At first I thought it a mistake—she would encourage his vacancies. But upon observing them both I revised my opinion. For I believe by the rapt expression on her face and the lightest movement of her lips and the far focus of her eyes that she was praying.

*　　*　　*

THE BOY'S CONDITION was diagnosed by Dr. Fulmer, at last, as the result of the father's spermatozoal frustration too hastily released. The doctor himself had cautioned Mauser that he should forbear from procreative attempts for at least a year, and that he should cleanse his system by a regimen of sexual emissions and releases that would come to no fruition, or human result. Fulmer pronounced the boy a tragical mistake, the effect of an aberrant spermatozoa deformed by the long practice of Karezza. There it was again! The vile practice! How I wept to find that by a twisted path my own reading and advice was the source of such pain in the outcome. Were we to know, to anticipate, how grave an implication might arrive from the slightest of our actions, I suppose we would not act at all. Still, what occurred seems unholy, ungodly, and the fact that I saw it develop as a retribution upon the meekness of a child, a small boy quickly growing, hopelessly, oh, monstrous, took away my faith. I simply don't have it anymore. Mauser ran to the church to beg forgiveness. Fleur prayed to what god or spirit she knew. But I rejected any deity who would so construct nature to fail. In fact, I cried shame. Shame on God! And I was not afraid to say it.

When the boy spun in circles for hours at a time. When his speech came out sideways. When his rage for sweet things overwhelmed us and especially at those times he went utterly tranced, void, blank, I made a calm promise to the deity that I should slap Him should we ever meet.

"So You'd best send me to the devil," I said at night, instead of uttering my usual prayer, "for I'll take You to task if You admit me to heaven. I'll try my very best to exact an explanation. I'd like one. I won't stop asking. Why did You do this? Why did You do this to a child?"

*   *   *

REINSTATED WITH the household, I had moved in my little Diablo, the Pomeranian who treated me with such contempt. Now I decided that I should train it to revise its attitude toward me and tried to withhold food, but that was impossible. The beast would starve before it would show affection. And I always thought dogs were incapable of turning face against one. So much for "merely" canine affection! I might have believed that I was too arduous a person to love, except that the boy had shown me different. He had changed my expectation and unlike Mauser I not only craved but understood that some return on my feelings should be mine.

That I was *not* so blighted a creature as I'd begun to accept was seconded, though not in so many words, by Fleur. Oh, many times it was obvious she had been drinking. She now tried to hide her consumption, but, to one who does not imbibe, the undertone of spirits is unmistakable. No matter how much Fleur gargled with orange flower water, I could tell. She put her arms around me, sometimes just to guide her faltering step. But other times she embraced me with true emotion, often when she witnessed how much I loved her child. She had a heart, no matter how she tried to hide it from her husband, a heart that stood both fast and passionate when it came to defending those she loved. I found out. There was an incident.

We took the boy by streetcar to the lake one afternoon. It was an adventure. We'd thrown off Fantan's guardianship and struck off on our own with an umbrella and a basket of food and drink. I knew, of course, there would be a flask of whiskey underneath the folded napkins. But I ignored my uneasy regret. My cure was a curse. I understood that. I tried to reason with her often, but today I decided to turn a blind eye. Anyway, what happened occurred before she'd even sipped a drop.

We'd walked out on the long dock to catch the fresh breeze, found a bench at the very end, and sat down there together to watch clouds. Fleur nicked her chin up into the sky. She pointed at things that way, with her face, her lips, the expression in her eyes. She never used her hands or fingers.

"My mother's name," she said.

I didn't understand.

"Anaquot. My mother's name. One of her names."

"Anaquot. It has a lovely sound. What does it mean?"

"Cloud."

To the west, in blazing white billows, the clouds were massing. Over us the most perfect, rounded, pillow puff shapes were arranged in a warm blue sky. Our boy was standing at the rail at the dock's end with his fishing pole, the hook baited with a bit of salt pork. At any moment, I was sure he'd catch a sunfish and I would shout for him, praise him high, and take the chance to gather him close. But the fish weren't biting or they didn't like salt pork. The sun struck our faces and arms. We grew lazy. We watched the clouds pass back and forth.

A man and woman came to the end of the dock and stood next to the boy looking out over the water. I saw them from the corner of my eye. Didn't register. Then something drew me to stare at the man's back and my heart crumpled like a mistaken drawing. I felt quite sick. It was the man who'd "done" the house of which Fleur was now mistress. It was the architect. I looked around wildly in a terror to escape, and met Fleur's eyes. She frowned and gripped my arm, seeing that there was something very wrong, and just as

I tried to gesture, to mouth the words, to indicate that I must hurry off or be discovered, he turned around. He and the woman—that is, the small, pretty, dark-haired, immaculately complexioned woman. Her figure was a graceful little arc. Her hair was cut in the latest fashion and she wore tiny webs of lace on her hands. She was the figure on top of a jewelry box.

"Why if it isn't Miss Gheen," he said, and then, just by the way my name was received by his companion, his sweetheart, his mistress I suppose, perhaps his fiancée, I knew the two of them had spoken of me together, before this moment.

"Ah, Miss Gheen!" The tiny woman glided up to me with the effortless movement of a dancer. Her face was all mocking curiosity. I understood at once that their conversation together had been at my expense, that I had been the butt of their fun together. Her hand was in his and I saw her squeeze it as if to say, *Watch me bait her. Watch this!*

"Miss Gheen, I've heard so very much about you," she simpered.

I stammered, my face flushing wildly. I wished to jump right off the dock!

"I believe you have some . . . history . . . with my husband-to-be . . ."

Suddenly her coo turned to a gurgle. She leaned backward and went off balance, tiptoed for purchase, and swung her little parasol in an ungainly fashion as Fleur stepped neatly into place between us. Fleur had apprehended the situation, perhaps not the entire history of my shame—that I'd tried an awkward seduction would have been impossible for her to know—but somehow she caught the gist of what was happening. She knew to stand where she did, and then step forward. And forward. Without speaking.

"Who are you?" The small woman gave a little shriek, and spun away from Fleur with a flustered wave. I was emboldened.

"I would like to introduce you to Mrs. John James Mauser," I said, from behind Fleur.

"Ah!" Weakly, the architect succumbed, cringed a little, and put out his hand with a smile he hoped would charm. He of course counted upon the good recommendations of those who held a mass of money, an unusual circumstance and soon to change, in fact, for John James Mauser. He wouldn't risk offending the friend of the wife of a powerful client, and pulled his little trick away from the scene with a scrape of apologies.

Watching, I felt a heady triumph sneak through the center of me, rise like bubbles from the bottom of a champagne bottle, until I blurted out a laugh. Fleur turned to me, her face a comical copy of the woman's sly and smug attempt to embarrass me. I was undone. We laughed together and then the boy, unknowing but only hearing us, joined in, raucous and funny all on his own. We couldn't stop laughing as we opened our basket, as we spread our little repast on the bench. We kept laughing—not that we spoke of what had happened—it was all mime between us. My pretend twirl of the arrogant lace parasol made us hoot. Fleur reeled herself along the railings in a hilarious caricature. For me it was, somehow, a blessed afternoon. My self-pity about my failure in love was erased. The absurd triumphed. I had a true connection, something quite beyond the pale of words. *If one accepts*, I thought later, as we drowsily swayed home on the streetcar. If one only accepts what is given! There could be afternoons of laughter. There could even be happiness. If one only accepts!

*　　*　　*

PERHAPS my understanding came about at Fleur's expense, for as I see it now, *she* was not happy. She was more trapped than in control, even with the position she had gained as Mauser's wife. Between the two of them, laughter ceased. There was a humming tension, an electric shadow. It was not a thing I wished to investigate or understand, but I had no choice in it once I placed myself firmly in the household. I would know the truth of their marriage whether or not I wanted to. I thought of course that the pain John James Mauser admitted to about the boy, the anguish that drove him to Holy Mass, was the source of all that was wrong between them. I had no idea, for instance, that Fleur knew that Mauser had wronged and stolen and gained his fabulous position in the first place by obtaining false holdings in northern Minnesota. I didn't think she knew he'd cut the last of the great pine forests there, thousands of acres, or that he'd left behind a world of stumps and then sold the land off cheap.

We had progressed to the point of speaking about it, Mauser and I, and I did tell him that I thought it a blessing that Fleur had no idea where his fortune had originated.

"Oh, but she does know," he said. We were sitting together in his library one night, and he was brooding over a bottle of old brandy he'd fetched from the cellar. He had asked me to sit with him. I felt there was something he wanted to tell me and there would be some roundabout way of getting at it.

"Fleur knows?"

"I'm just one of an army of swindlers and scavengers," he laughed shortly, giving me a long look underneath his eyebrows. "I've got the misfortune, perhaps, to have understood at last what

I've done. She has let me know full well the misery I left behind. She has told me that she expects I'll sell this house, that I'll give her the automobile she covets, and our son. Our son! She tells me that she expects that I will restore her land and give her all of my money."

I thought I'd heard what I'd heard, but I made him repeat the whole thing.

"Why, you can't do that," I said, oddly moved by her faith. I think I spoke somewhat wistfully, as though it was possible, after all, for a man like Mauser to go broke through the exercise of sheer moral principles.

"Of course not, but she doesn't understand. Even if I did have the money, which I don't anymore, I could hardly make restitution to a people who've become so depraved. I know the folly of those people up there now! The old type, the old warrior type, they are gone. Only the wastrels, the dregs of humanity left, only the poor toms have survived. Even she left. I point that out to her. The reservations are ruined spots and may as well be sold off and all trace of their former owners obliterated. That's my theory. Let the Indians drift into the towns and cities or subsist where they will. Thinking their tribes will ever be restored is sheer foolishness. There's nothing left!"

Mauser shook his head, and puffed away on his cigar to form a melancholy cloud that stopped above his head.

"I don't think she wants to kill me anymore," he said. "That's one thing. She can't. In some interior way—I cannot grasp it, I don't even experience it—she has developed a form of love for me. I call it love, anyway, though I suspect it is more like pity. Kindness. Some honor in her that won't permit my death at her hand.

I meditate on this—it's strange! I could feel her hatred of me change with the birth of the boy."

"She hated you?" I said this in an aghast tone, but a split second later I was of course not surprised, thinking, yes, of course she hated you. She came here hating you. I see that now. Her dark figure on that white, white day. A cipher. A keyhole. I was the one who admitted her into this house. It was no accident. She found you because she wished to destroy you but then she started healing you and found that once she'd healed you she could not kill you. For who can destroy what one has put back together with such care? And then the boy—you after all are the father of her son. She loves him. Therefore, she can't kill you. So she is trapped. I said this last sentence aloud. He did not acknowledge it, though I know he heard.

"Of course she hated me. She came here to skin me and had a very sharp knife to do it with. But the whiskey got her, as it does so many of her people. It will waste her in a few years. Already, she's gotten careless. It won't be long."

"How can you speak in such a heartless fashion?" I was angry. "You profess to love her, and yet you will watch her be destroyed."

"There is no helping her, don't you see? The stuff is poison to them. It's their downfall. They'd have beaten us back and kept their lands if it wasn't for the liquor. They can't help it. One taste, one teaspoon of it, and they're utterly doomed."

Now he forgot to smoke his sad cigar. Real feeling seized him. His eyes whelmed with felt tears and he looked at me with something like appeal.

"I almost wish she would kill me," he said. "Sometimes I do. I cannot watch the wreck she will become. She's caught me somehow." He touched the breast of his jacket, softly, with the tips of his fingers. "It isn't just her face, either, or the figure she cuts. It isn't that I married her for notoriety, as some say, but only that I couldn't bear not to have her near. God," his voice went ragged. "I had to have her and I swear to you there was no other way. Only now do I understand that I had to get near something in her that I can't know, some pure space, something that I went up north to have and only ended up destroying. It is the same with her," he nearly wailed, and then I thought, oh, he feels sorry for *himself*. He regained control and spoke with a surface sincerity. "I am a greedy man. I have always been a greedy man and always wanted to live like this"—he waved his arm around the oak-paneled room—"and now I do, for the next few months anyway. After that, I think . . ."

"What," I said, knowing this was where he'd wanted to lead me. "Tell me the worst!"

"I think it's all gone. I think you must find yourself a new place to live. Go back to your sister."

I took that in. The fire crackled in the hearth. I gestured to my glass and he poured out fingers of brandy for us both.

"Fleur is my sister, now," I said. "I think I'll cast my lot with her."

Mauser looked at me in astonishment. His mouth actually dropped open. He gave a bark of laughter. "She'll go back! She'll go back there to live, I suppose! I have nothing. I plan to leave the country with all that I can pry from my bankers before the great rout, and she refuses to come with me."

"She probably misses her family," I said sharply to him, trying to fight off my appalled shock. The world, indeed, was breaking apart. I could function only by remaining dry and allowing my old vinegar into my voice.

"Her family?" Now he laughed a good deal longer. "She hasn't any. She's the last of them."

"Well, she's got me now," I said, rising, rustling my skirt. I seemed to grow taller in my own skin. "If she'll have me, she's got Miss Gheen."

ELEVEN

Dog Love

Nanapush

𝓜ARGARET SLOWLY and methodically began to gather the materials that she would use in making the medicine dress. Just as she had said, nothing upon it could be made by a whiteman, which was not easy as chimookomaanag popped up everywhere—stole the land next door and put a farm on it, walked the agency town's streets, even prayed in our missionizing church. Margaret couldn't use glass beads to decorate her dress, but as in the old days she must use deer clackers, teeth, quills, and the bones of small birds. This required the painstaking hunting of those animals, which I did with a good will, as I thought my efforts might redeem me from the terrible mistake of the snare. Bine, or partridge, sat juicy in the comfort of the tree

131

branches. I knew how to catch them with a wire hooked to the top of a long pole. Plucked and roasted, the birds were delicate meat, sweet and tender. I also let it be known that I was collecting these bird bones, and would be glad to clean up the remnants of various partridges cooked throughout the reservation.

These were good times. These were the sorts of jobs I liked— catching food, visiting about, eating roast partridges. Whenever I returned with a load of quills or bird bones, Margaret rewarded me in ways I can only dream of, now, looking back. Gizhe Manito had smiled on me then and smoothed my way. I had lived through great sorrows and, as though to reward me, I was given for that short time all I needed for happiness. But such times are brief. We should never think happiness will last. We shouldn't chase it, for the faster we do the faster it recedes. I was happy all through the making of that dress, so I suppose that proves its power. But maybe, with Margaret, with the treasure of our love, I tried too hard to hold on to what is only fleeting, and fragile, and I destroyed it with my clumsy ways.

IF ONLY Nector hadn't come home again, things would perhaps have gone on forever in a pleasant dream. I wanted to live in love until Margaret and I faded into the next world, worn smooth and transparent by the rubbing of skin on skin. I wanted nothing but the happiness of falling asleep in each other's arms, craved only the calm discriminations of old age manaa. But there was Nector one afternoon, sitting on a rock beside the door eating bannock. Margaret beamed down on him like the moon. I was glad to see Nector as if he were my own son, for we understood things in a similar fashion. He was smart, and for sure, he'd grown up to arrange the features of his mother and father in the best possible combination. All the girls admired his looks. It was my task to keep him from falling prey to vanity—an uncle's responsibility.

"All that manaa you're having is making you thin," I said, "the bones are poking through your skin. Most unattractive."

"Just one bone counts," he glanced down, "with women."

"More like a rope," I said, critical, "a short little piece."

"Yours is," laughed Nector, stuffing a huge grease-covered chunk of pikwezhigan into his mouth. "Bread and lard make you hard," he mocked in a singsong voice.

"Neither one of you have much to brag of," said Margaret, sitting down with us. "Women come to you out of pity." But she smiled at me from the corner of her eyes to let me know that this was not the case. My heart swelled up. That moment was very dangerous. I experienced a collision of desires. First, I wanted to make the moment last with Margaret, in the hope it would lead to other things. She had been generous two nights ago. Would my luck hold out? Second, I wanted to keep on teasing Nector, for his own good. Third, what was it? I couldn't remember. An old man's thoughts fly in and out of his head. Oh yes. There was something I had to avoid, like a treacherous rock. It could rip the bottom of my boat. But it was hidden. I couldn't recall in that moment exactly what I was attempting to avoid and so like someone trying to steer away I instead disremembered the place and was drawn right to it.

"You're pretty good at snaring women," I said to Nector, "but you can't keep them, I hear."

As soon as I said the word, I remembered with a jolt of panic, *snare, snare, snare!* Immediately, my brain spun. I tried to throw down a distracting piece of nonsense about the famous quality of

Margaret's bannock, praised it loud, out of desperation, but Nector had already seized on the word I feared.

"Snaring?" he began to laugh.

"I can't hold myself back!" I cried, lunging over him, "I must have yet another piece of this bread. Old woman, you have a way with your cooking that—"

"Snares you every time," said Nector, feeling hilarious. "That reminds me—"

"Gego!" I cried out, hoping he'd recall that I had requested his silence on the long-ago incident I knew he'd just remembered. "Aaargh!" I fell upon the ground, as though unconscious, and began to writhe and moan. They disregarded me except to find in my agony a source of humor.

"Look how the old man pretends he's poisoned. Very funny. He does this all the time," said Margaret fondly.

"He's a sly one," said Nector, approving of me, too. "Remember how he once snared Clarence Morrissey? He showed me how to set the wire and the two of us waited in the bush until we caught the dog. The Morrissey nearly choked to death, but found a toehold at the last moment. Of course, back then the old man told me to keep it a secret."

Nector looked uncertainly at Margaret, whose mouth had dropped open and then slowly shut to a line. "I was just a boy," he went on, nervously, "but now, what does it matter?" Nector noticed I had gone stiff on the ground. I was playing dead.

"Look, he's playing dead," he tried to change Margaret's focus. "Convincing, isn't he?"

"It won't be play for long" was Margaret's answer.

Then silence. I waited for her blows to fall upon me where I lay defenseless and stupid. But she did nothing, which made me even more afraid. I opened my eyes a crack, and my terror was confirmed. From the set of her mouth and the flash in her eyes, I knew she understood all and was reserving punishment. Mere browbeating, tongue lashing, ass kicking, and starvation of an old man would not be enough. She gave a chilly little grin, rose, and turned her back on the two of us.

"It is time for me to rest my old bones," I said in despair. Then I crawled into the corner of the house and burrowed under a heap of blankets. I covered my face, bit my tongue, and turned to the wall. There, I prayed to the spirit of the turtle.

"Come help me," I called on my dodem, the mekinak. "Not to stick out my head, my arms, my feet, my tail or niinag." I thought that if I could only contain myself and stay beneath the covers, Margaret might progress to the end of her anger and find there a morsel of tenderness. The good priest tells us that miracles are part of ordinary life, but not for the lazy or the wicked, and I was both according to the Catholics. As it turned out, I was bound to suffer. To absorb a hard medicine. And Margaret knew exactly what to cook up for the poor old man and how to deliver it most drastically.

So I had snared her. She would snare me right back. We both knew that she was doing it and both of us knew why, but neither of us had the courage to dismantle the barrier of hard sticks, pointed words, and prickles of jealousy that soon tangled like deep bush between us. I knew she had divined the true prey of that snare I'd set, figured out the reason I tried to kill him, and decided to resurrect my jealousy and use Shesheeb as a weapon. Although I was aware of her ploy, I couldn't help her scorn from cutting, or the thorns of her words from piercing deep.

One night, she hummed in an irritating manner, beneath her

breath. "Ninimoshe," she finally let me hear her singing, "sweetheart, little duck, speak softly, for my old man will hear you creeping underneath my blanket."

Of course, after that I tossed all night, at each little noise, imagining the absurd picture of the greasy old duck sneaking into our cabin. Now that she slept across the room from me, such a thing was remotely possible. I began to sleep by the door, but then I feared the window. The upshot was I got no sleep at all.

"People say they know the old man down the road," she said to me slyly the next day, "but not as I do. His powers are significant. Why, he can turn himself into a fly, buzz about, listen in on people."

I tried to bite my tongue, to keep my temper from flaring up. A fly! Saaah! That time, I succeeded. But other times I did not. She laughed, now, when I insisted on accompanying her to Holy Mass. For years, she had begged my presence, hoping to convert one more soul for Father Damien and lure me into a church marriage. Now she refused to let me walk beside her.

"Don't follow!" She whacked the earth with her walking stick, and glared. "I'll kick you sideways if you sneak after me!"

I soon grew to think it would be better for me to live in the woods with the bears than endure the insults she heaped on my head in the form of admiring remarks about Shesheeb. She boasted of the old man's hunting skills, and how he always had fresh game—waawaashkeshi or mooz.

"Never gopher! Never things I've seen you eat!"

"What would you know? You never cook for me anymore." I tried to make myself meek and pitiful. "You'll come home from Holy Mass one day and find me dried up in the corner, starved to death."

"Go snare something then," she said, heartless.

She walked out laughing at me, came back with bird bones for her dress. I didn't ask where she got them, only if I could help her dye them red with the bark of speckled alder I'd gathered in atonement.

"You?" She looked at me and sniffed, as though I were covered with moowan. "You might interfere with the dress's healing properties."

In other words, she didn't trust that I wouldn't contaminate her medicine dress. This cut me deeper than anything she'd done so far and I let myself be naked in my speech.

"I've got nothing in my heart but love for you."

"Nothing in your pants either."

And with a cruel laugh, she sat against the shady side of the cabin to work on her dress, which after all this time was just about finished. I must admit, she was very patient and did a good job on it. The dress was made of a moosehide she'd pounded and stretched and rubbed to a velvet softness. She'd used raspberry leaf and root dyes to color the bird bones, and unlike the harsh, bright glare of the trader's beads, these soft pinks and purples put roses in that woman's cheeks. I said so.

"Don't touch" was all she answered. "My roses have pickers so long they could pierce your heart and kill you."

I watched the colors reflect into her face as she sewed that afternoon. She used a fish bone for a needle, sinew for thread. I crept close to her, thinking that maybe the medicine dress would do its healing work and bring us together, but the opposite happened.

"My, my," she clucked her tongue, her eyes sparking with malicious fire, "I'm dizzy. That old man down the road gave me a sip of wine!"

There comes a time when you reach the last bitter drop that your gullet can hold. That was it. Her words filled me with such hot rage that I had to ice my feelings instantly, or I'd explode. I imagined packing heavy snow around my heart, and made my choice. That was it. I'd had enough. I started walking down the road. She wanted wine? I'd bring wine. I could get it for her. I knew where. Sister Hildegarde Anne made the parish communion wine and kept it in the convent cellar, which opened from a side door with a flimsy bolt that had been placed there years ago, right after I'd taken a few bottles and had a ripping good time. That bolt could easily be jiggled out of place. This time, I'd steal the whole cask, I decided. I'd bring it back to our cabin and have a party with my sweetheart. She wanted wine? I'd get wine. Our love would be just like old times, way back when. We'd have a bush dance for just the two of us! My stride quickened and in spite of myself my heart thawed. My thoughts pumped with hope and a young man's zeal. Once I made town, I visited around, chewed snuff, collected a few more tiny bones for my woman's dress. I killed time until it was dark, then crept close to the convent. Crouched beneath an open window, I heard the nuns say their nightly prayers.

"God comfort you, my daughters," I whispered as they doused their lamps and each made her way to a lonely cell. "May you each get laid."

After I pronounced my blessing, I waited until they slept and then I slipped up to the cellar door and quietly fiddled with the catch. I used a splinter of partridge bone jammed in the crack between the door and frame to ease the bolt from its casing. It didn't take long. The cool winey air, earth scented and moldy, rushed at my face as I slipped inside. I lighted a match and by its flare saw that the casks were there for the taking. I hefted the first little wooden keg onto my shoulder, eased out of the cellar quietly, and set out for home. It had been a very long time since I'd tasted wine. In my youth, it made me foolish, stole my brain, and left a bannock between my ears. Drink caused me to sing and gamble, to fight, to chase women who belonged to other men, and even for a short time to forsake the pipe that my father gave me. Liquor did not get the best of my life, but I knew well its powers. I had taken no wine or liquor for many years because I had experienced its evils. And yet, at that moment, all I could think of was its delights—the sour and delicious odor of the fumes that the keg exuded made my mouth water. The air was heavy and growing heavier. I set the cask down and took a rest beside the road. If I should have a drink, I thought, my load would be one drink lighter. So sitting there, in the dark, I took my first drink in many years.

The wine went down easy. The keg went back up slow. An old and familiar warmth burned in my gut and then swirled up around my heart. Again, I started off for home. The moon was up and just bright enough for me to make out the road. As I walked on, the warm thrill of wine reached my tongue and untied it. I found myself singing an old love song. *You are paddling away, my sweetheart. But I will come after you. Marry me tonight.* Into my thoughts came pictures of the happiness that Margaret and I would feel once we'd put aside all of our foolish attempts to best each other at the jealous game of revenge. Do you hear me correctly? Do you understand what I am telling you? What began as a scheme between Margaret and me to get the best of each other ended up getting the best of us both. Revenge ran away with us, and then it turned around and ran over us. Flattened us good. It is also the case, and I know you've remarked it, that my struggle with love and wine paralleled in some ways the journey of Fleur on this earth. We both were tempted, and succumbed. This happens even to strong persons, and perhaps it is most dangerous of all for us to stumble. For we are subject to the worst shame, those of us who are too proud. It is hard for us to admit that we can be tricked by the same ordinary firewater that tricks the common idiot. But the booze makes no distinction, and the smarter we are, the more elaborate our reasons for guzzling.

THE KEG grew heavy again, n'dawnis. I stopped on the road. I took a drink to lighten it, and then another, and then perhaps one too many, for I stumbled as I set off once more. At one point, near dawn, I woke to find myself curled up around my friend, the keg, right in the middle of the road. I'd slept peacefully and was grateful not to have been run over by a wagon. I took another drink. By then the cask was so light I had no trouble reaching the cabin. Margaret greeted me at the doorway. Her look was foul.

"I was up all night, worried! I thought a bear got you!"

"Ah," I put the wine cask down and covered my heart with the palms of my hands, overcome. "My love! You worried about me?"

She regarded the wine keg suspiciously. "What did you bring, akiwenzii?"

"That is a peace offering," I said. "It is wine. You told me the black duck tried a sip of wine to win your womanly favors. I thought I'd do him one better and offer you a cask . . . or most of it."

Margaret looked down at the keg, frowning, then kicked. It rolled, nearly empty. "Most of it?" she said. For a moment I also feared she recognized it as belonging to the nuns' cellar. But she only shook her head and hid—perhaps, but I could not be sure of it—a little smile. It had been a very long time since she'd drunk any wine herself, and maybe she was thinking, just as I had thought, what would be the harm of it when we were each so near the end of our days? I poured a tin cup full and offered it to her. For a moment, she looked tempted, but then she knocked the cup out of my hands. "Your damn keg's nearly empty! You drank it all!" I retrieved the cup midair—a drunk is capable of such tricks—and downed it in one defiant gulp without a drop spilled.

"I'm a medicine dancer, according to my dream," said Margaret, standing proud and straight as her old bones would allow, "I won't take the ishkode wabo, old man." She paused, then bent close to me. "Just let me smell it." She took a whiff. "Those were the days," she said, a bit mournfully. Much of her anger toward me seemed to have dissolved at the sight of the lengths I was willing to go to win her favor. She knew how many times and for how many years I refused a drink, up until she drove me to the edge. And as well, perhaps the dress helped. She had been working on it when I arrived, and now she held it up against her—a soft, dun-colored, plum-beaded old-time dress. Finished.

"Put the dress on," I urged, hoping to coax her into the spirit of authentic forgiveness. "Let me see you in it!"

I leaned back against a tree, poured the tin cup full again, and watched as she shook off her old cotton majigoode, stood a moment in only her shift. Carefully, she lowered the new medicine dress onto herself and then quickly stalked inside, fetched her eagle fan from its strap on the wall. While she was in there, she braided her hair and painted two black dots at the corners of her eyes. Then she emerged from the cabin and stood regal and queenly before me with a farseeing look of wisdom on her face. I had to stagger around and lower myself to sit against the tree, otherwise I would have fallen over from the simple beauty of the shock. Margaret. Rushes Bear. Great-granddaughter of old Medicine Dress. My love. She looked like a woman out of a dream, a spirit lady from the sky, an old-time ogichidaa-ikwe, a proud grandmother for the ages. Tears stung my eyes, and then I overflowed and wept out loud.

"My precious sweetheart, are you a vision?"

"Of sorts," said Margaret, carried away just a little herself.

She turned around and around, wishing she could catch more of a reflection of herself than the picture in the tiny scrap of mirror we owned. I tried my best to reflect her, using words. How proudly your bosom thrusts out, I said. And your waist is slim as a girl's. Your braids are coming along nicely, too, I observed. That was not exactly true. Hers had never grown back properly. They were stubby and gray. Mine were longer. It didn't hurt to say a good word, however, and she appreciated it. If we had stopped right there, if she had taken off the dress, we would have ended up happily together for the day and on into the night, I am convinced. But my guardian spirits weren't with me. My love luck failed. For once I fetched the drum and sang for her, and once she started to dance, Margaret ruined the effect. Though the dress was magnificent, my lady love was barely competent. Maybe less. Clumsy, I'd have to call her, out of step, out of balance.

"I guess I never saw you dance before," I mumbled, shocked and dizzied by her bobbing missteps.

"Sure you have," said Margaret, "many times. As you remember, I was head female dancer years ago."

"Mii nange," I mumbled, not sure of anything. "You're tipping!"

"You're tipping, old shkwebii," she was irritated. "You can't see straight."

But she was wrong. There were two of her hopping in as miserable a crow step as a white woman. It hurt to watch.

"Dagasana, please," I shielded my eyes and I asked her very gently, as careful with my words as could be, "let me put on the dress and show you how to do it!'

She stopped dancing with a jerk, drove her hands to her hips, and glared. She puffed out her cheeks and looked as though she might explode in a cloud of bird-bone beads and tattered bashkwegin. Then she flipped her fan and suddenly laughed, harsh and mean, "I'd love to see you in a dress, old crazy. The medicine is strong in this one. Maybe it will sober you up!"

"I don't care about that, lady love," I said to her in my most sincere voice. "I just want to make sure you don't make a fool of yourself."

At that, she stood still and almost ripped the dress off her body.

"Here"—she thrust it at me—"you be the fool!"

The wine was treating me well at that point. I felt my own dignity rise up in me. "Give me the fan, too, old lady, and get ready for some old-time traditional woman dancing. You take the drum! My feet move light as a doe's!"

"Oh yai!" She was outraged, I knew it, but I thought to win her over with my patient instruction. I tried my best not to anger her, and started easily, keeping to the beat with what I thought was wondrous perfection. My steps were subtle. I moved like water. I could feel how well I floated around on the grass of the yard, and lost myself in the beat although the drum had stopped.

I could feel her eyes upon me, full of unwilling admiration, at least I thought so. But when I chanced to look around, at last, expecting to collect praise and take in the pride on her face, I was surprised to find that I was quite alone. She was gone. I was miserably wounded, but only for a second, and in the next instant my suspicions grabbed me. Off to Shesheeb's, no doubt! I put her eagle fan back in the house and started through the bush, intending to have it out with him at last.

The leaves grew thick. Roots tripped me. Raspberry pickers scratched my arms and grabbed my ankles, but I held to my path. I skirted the scene of recent disaster, the sprung snare, and eventually found the clearing around the little house that once had belonged to Iron Sky and now sheltered sly Shesheeb. It was a scene of calm. He hadn't kept the place up though, at all. The roof was already sagging. The yard was a mess of garbage. A thread of smoke twisted in the still air. My heart squeezed—was he inside the house with Margaret? I was just about to rush the cabin when the door opened and the old man emerged, hunched over, groping his way into the sun. He turned his face up to the light, squinting. It relieved me to see that he was alone.

So this was Shesheeb. Well, he was not much! Where was his power? His medicine? I made a small movement and he turned his head. His hearing, at least, was very keen.

As long as I was discovered, I stepped forward and presented myself before him. I didn't expect to react so strong and quick, but my blood rose, hot, and my heart beat murderously. I could hardly contain my hate. There were no words I needed to say. There was no message. I stood entirely still in the sun and allowed him to examine me with what eyesight he had, to recognize me and in so doing recognize his crime. I waited. He blinked his white eyes, opaque and cloudy with cataract. His face had collapsed around his nose. His nostrils quivered, his chin strained toward me, he tried to sense all he could, to hear the beating of my heart. His rag of white hair hung to his waist and he wore a strange purple vest made of some heavy flowered material. His pants were filthy and held up by rope. He was nothing to look at and didn't even have shoes on so I could see that his feet were filthy clawed things, splayed and frightening. I could not imagine what Margaret saw in him—in fact, it was now clear that all along she'd just been trying to pique my jealousy. I edged backward. I now wished I'd never come to make any sort of challenge. Best to leave a sleeping duck lie in its dirty nest.

"Who are you?" Shesheeb asked, at last. "You beauty, have you come to tempt me?"

I stepped back, startled, as you can imagine. I had entirely forgotten, in my examination of the old man, that I was dressed as a quite attractive woman. I said nothing, though sudden laughter welled inside of me and I was hard put to contain it. That's when I got an idea. I'd get the old fake to fall in love with me. I'd torture his heart! I'd make him beg for my attentions, then abandon him and have a good laugh with Margaret. Perhaps I'd kill him and eat him just like he devoured my sister. I didn't dare use my voice.

"Ahhh," I sighed. Just a little sigh, like some wind caught in the branches. He stepped closer. His nose twitched back and forth.

"Piindegen! Come into my cabin and have a cup of tea with me," he cried. "There's a chill in the air today."

"Mmmm," I crooned. I had to agree with him. The tea sounded just the thing. So I entered his evil nest.

145

Inside, the place was chaos. Piles of junk everywhere. Bones in one corner, rags in another. No place to sit and barely room to stand up. Shesheeb hobbled to the stove and poked some embers, added a new bit of wood. There was a mashed old iron pot on top of the stove with some oily tea in it. This, he tried to heat up. Next to the pot was set a can with scum in the bottom—soup maybe. His supper, no doubt. I couldn't help but gloat and in my gloating wonder at my luck in holding on to a woman who kept things comfortable for me, cooked my food, and never let my tea grow cold and unpleasant-tasting like the tea that Shesheeb gave me now. I took a drink. Though it was only half warmed up, still the tea seemed to fill my bones with a slow, hot, blooming sensation. I finished the stuff and then, in spite of myself, I wanted more. Which was when it hit me. *He'd* hit me. Shesheeb had medicined me and I'd fallen for it! He was smiling now, just a little smile, private and knowing. Here, I'd felt sorry for him. I had let him lure me into his cabin where he could play on his strengths, where he knew his way around. I was suddenly sure that he knew exactly who I was and had planned this moment. Perhaps he'd even drawn me to him through the woods!

Though blind and decrepit, he had power. I must watch myself.

"Ooooh," I trailed the sound as I put down my snakish brew. Shesheeb actually shuddered a little, as if he found me irresistible. He reached around behind himself and picked up a hand drum and drumstick with knowing authority.

"May I play a little song for you?" he said, his voice a slippery whine. Without waiting for my answer, he struck the drum. "Niimin," he ordered. Without wanting to at all, I stood. Completely against my will, I began to dance just as he directed. Quietly, with even movements, in exact time with the drum and the strange song he sang whose words I still cannot remember, I bobbed in the shadowy mess of Shesheeb's cabin. I tried to stop myself, to still my legs, to make my feet heavy and quit. But I could not and the movement of my body soon filled me with horror as nothing else had ever done. I was quickly becoming exhausted, too, reeling from the wine I'd drunk and the long stumble back from town. Still my feet rose and stamped down. My legs trod. I jigged. If I danced much longer, I knew that my old heart would burst, but as long as Shesheeb sang his song and struck his drum I was caught, shuffling one foot to the next. I felt myself going, bright spots shifting across my vision, pains shooting through my lungs. I would have died right there, I know it, if my love medicine had not unexpectedly showed up and worked itself.

Shesheeb's dog, most surely not allowed in the cabin, bounded suddenly in and greeted its master. With a cry, almost of fear, Shesheeb tried to shoo it out. It had been a good while since I'd treated that dog, by accident, but even though sweat dripped into my eyes and stung me I could see that dog clearly enough to recognize the poor runt, the sad little outcast fellow who'd been quick enough to lap up my love powder. Now, to my surprise, Shesheeb became flustered by its presence. Could it be that the dog, whom in fact I'd heard rumored was the slyest stud yet seen on the reservation, was somehow in the habit of intimidating Shesheeb? The old duck beat the drum a little faster. The dog groveled and licked his knee. He tried to kick the dog away and keep on singing at the same time, but suddenly it was obvious that my love powder was too strong. The dog fell into a sudden passion, hunkered over, and began to make love to Shesheeb's old shin with a vicious ardor that cared not for sharp words or strikes of the drumsticks or wild blows. That dog humped away like the devil and broke Shesheeb's rhythm with its thrusts. Released, I pushed past the dangerous old medicine man and staggered into the sunlight and freedom of the yard and then the woods, for I did not even pause, but plunged forward in a stupor of relief until I reached the main road.

There, I stopped. Which way to turn, home or town? Either way, I had nothing to lose. What was there for me now but more shame and misery? Why not go down, to the bottom of my life, all the way? It occurred to me that in the nuns' cellar other casks of wine were stored—cool, dark, and safe. My steps went sideways, as though drawn in that direction by a call. Surely, I thought, finding myself back on the road to town, the chance to divert wine from the lips of the priest and parish to the gullet of Nanapush was far, far too good to pass up. So I continued down the long, dusty road.

I slept the afternoon away in the cemetery, and woke at dusk raging with a deep and unbearable thirst. I'd been thirsty before, but never like this. My thirst was a gripping force that both made my head swim and keenly focused my brain. It was a powerful longing that alerted my whole body to one intention.

I agonized for an hour at least in my mystic dryness before I thought it safe once again to approach the nuns' residence. Again, as before, I listened to the nuns' prayers beneath their window, and dispensed my fervent wish for their well-being through manaa. Again, I crept to the cellar's entrance and opened it with great care, attempting not to let the boards creak. I slid into the gloom and felt my way with enormous care to the shelf that held the kegs of wine. And then, just as I embraced the round barrel, and just as I hoisted it in a strength born of momentary joy, a crash resounded behind me. The cellar door slammed shut. I froze. A woman's voice rang out. Sister Hildegarde Anne!

"Wine thief!" she cried in triumph. "I've trapped you! There is no way out. When morning comes, we'll see who you are! As if we don't know," she said sarcastically, "you old degenerate."

I heard a heavy board slide into place outside, barring the door. Crowing, jangling her keys, telling me to rest well because the reservation drunk tank would surely be a noisier place than the cellar, she left. I was alone once more, but far less disturbed by my capture than you might think. The main question that immediately entered my mind was this: How much of the parish wine could I drink before morning? How many kegs could I enjoy?

I CAN'T TELL YOU the number, to this day. I don't remember that night after the first hour or so that I spent chugging my fill. I suppose I was happy, but I must content myself with other people's memory. Father Damien says that he woke in the middle of the night convinced a powwow was taking place in the convent. I sang and danced, I know that. I was a one-man powwow, I think. The next morning, I was laid out cold when the Pukwans came and got me. When I woke in the stinking jailhouse, I was confused by my surroundings. Gradually, I was able to place myself. Our drunk tank at the time was no more than one side of a log cabin barricaded off from the other half, which the Pukwans proudly called their headquarters. Both sides were exactly the same except that theirs had a three-legged table, the legless side supported by a crate, and on the wall a rack of antlers that held an ancient shotgun. The floors of both sides were dirt and the walls were plain log, the bark scraped off in strips. My side smelled worse of piss, as well as the rank heaves of earlier drunks. The only light came through slots near the roof and the front door, which was habitually left open so that the flies could travel freely in and out. I was shocked by a dipper of cold water splashed hard in my face, and I clenched my eyes shut. Another dipper of water stung me.

"Enough!" I put my hand up and struggled to sit. I was hampered, it seemed, by a sheet wound around my legs.

"Come look at the mindimooyenh," yelled one Pukwan to the other.

I staggered to my feet, tried to walk, tripped and rolled out the door into dazzling light.

"How did this woman's dress get on me, my brothers?" I asked the Pukwans, sincerely puzzled.

"You pulled it over your fat head," said Edgar. Then, with relish, he added, "Do you know what today is?"

"Today," I said, thinking as quickly as my throbbing old brain would allow, "is the day we dress as women."

Both Pukwans burst into howls and sneers of derision.

"His brain has for sure flipped over in his skull," they agreed. "He has forgotten this is the day of the council meeting."

They were right, I had forgotten. This was the morning I was to present the plan I had worked so hard on to everyone who cared to attend the big meeting. As the tribal chairman, I was supposed to preside, and then call a vote on whether to accept the large settlement of money that was offered should we only leave our scrap of land.

"Lend me clothes," I begged the Pukwans, instantly doubling the volume of their hilarity. When they refused, I drew myself up straight and tried to reclaim my dignity.

"Well, if you won't give me clothes," I said, brushing at the skirt of the dress, "at least let me fix myself up. Give me a comb, a mirror, and a basin of water. A little rouge wouldn't do me any harm, either."

"Holy Jesus!" Their mirth increased and became almost unbearable. They found the items I'd requested. As they watched me braid my hair in perfect plaits, pull out my straggling beard hairs, smooth my eyebrows, and put some color into my cheeks, they were so wretchedly overcome with the humor of it all that they didn't bother to charge me with disorderly conduct, but merely waved me out the door while they convulsed like children in each other's arms.

If only I had not been so thorough in my demonstration for Margaret's benefit! If only I had worn my other clothing underneath! Unfortunately, I investigated and found I'd brazenly stripped right down to my skin. Although I was horrified at my situation, I had to admit that I felt pretty good in Margaret's dress—it was soft, and the air was cool, flowing up against me from underneath. Also, from what I saw in the mirror, it was becoming to me. I didn't look half bad. Still, I had no idea what I could possibly do to maintain my position of respect once I appeared before everyone assembled at the meeting. I thought of two people on the way, whose clothes I might beg, but they weren't home. Doubtless, they were waiting for me with the others at the powwow arbor, ready to decide the entire future of our tribe.

The day was splendid, a day of blue sky and puffy little clouds, the kind of day which on any other occasion I would spend catching fish, picking berries, setting snares, or just poking around in the bush. It was so beautiful, in fact, that in spite of my dismal prospects, I just had to stop and say a special prayer of thanks to the creator of us all, who had taken such pains in providing just the right amount of breeze, and tinted the sunlight an inspiring transparent golden color. Lost in praise, I hardly noticed that I was near the trading store, where at that hour people sat outside gossiping about whomever might happen by. A family of tourists who had come to the reservation to find some photo-worthy Indians spotted me, standing stock-still in the road.

"There's one!" I turned to see a man dragging his wife and children from their automobile. I started walking away at a quick, yet dignified pace, but they hurried after me. I tried to run, but the dress bound my legs and the family quickly surrounded me, asking to take a photograph.

"You're the first one we've met wearing a colorful costume!" cried the woman. "Would you mind standing still?" I had no choice, as two large children suddenly gripped me by the shoulder and arms, pinning me upright. I felt the young boy startle as he saw me close up.

"She's an ugly old woman though, isn't she, Mama!"

"Hush," the mother said.

"Ugly?" I am embarrassed to say this, but the boy's remark hurt my vanity.

"Get your hands off me," I cried, but the children's hands pinched harder. They were strong as little cows, and although I attempted to struggle, they held me fast with big grins pasted to their faces. I changed my tactics.

"Truly, I must be going now," I humbly begged the parents. "I must take my leave. So let us all stand together for our picture." I gestured to Zozed Bizhieu, who stood amazed with speculation on the steps of the trader's store.

"Ombe omaa, Zozed," I called, "take a photo of us together! Tell me exactly when you're going to push the button!"

Zozed put down her bundle, and I arranged myself in the middle of the family.

"On the count of three," Zozed called out, "bezhig, niizh, niswi . . ."

With an agile move, just as she clutched the camera, I turned around, bent over, and lifted the dress over my buttocks. While the parents were still in shock, I righted myself swiftly and did a rousing and educational French cancan dance, an anatomy lesson that enlightened the amazed children until the mother recovered her wits, put her hands across the children's eyes, and screamed. Before the father could gather himself and punish me, I fled. Cross-country through the bush, uphill, toward the arbor, I sprinted, not chancing the road. All the way there I prayed and I sang for those children, hoping I had not confused them too thoroughly by revealing a man's equipment underneath a woman's skirts.

THERE WAS nothing for it, I counseled myself, but to go forward boldly and rely on inspiration. When I reached the arbor, I strode to the center of the dance ground, and instead of skulking and cringing in shame, I threw open my arms. I turned in a circle and let people gawk and chatter and react with owlish surprise while my brain worked in a fever. When their speculation died away and they fell silent in anticipation, I opened my mouth. I didn't know what I'd say. I was surprised to hear my words flow into the air, but even more, I was surprised to see that people slowly lost their expressions of amusement and mirth, and regarded me with an increasingly serious composure. As close as I can remember, here are the words that emerged.

"Friends, relatives, nindinawemaganidok, I am Nanapush, witness of disasters, friend of folly, a man of the turtle clan, a son of old Mirage whose great deeds brought our people back to life. I am one hundred percent pure Anishinaabeg and I speak my language and the English both. But today, that English language tastes foul, tastes rancid in my mouth, for it is the language in which we are, as always, deceived. Lies are manufactured in that English language. All the treaties are written in English, are they not? In its wording our land is stolen. All the labels on the whiskey bottles are in English, do you agree? When we drink from the English bottles we piss away our minds. How can we speak English when the truth lies heavy on our Ojibwe tongues?

"You have made free with your laughter. You have subjected this dress, which my wife has made, to derision and to ridicule. You have satisfied yourselves at the expense of this piece of clothing I am wearing. Now let us speak of where it came from—the spirits. Let us speak of the decision before us—which also involves the spirits. Let us speak of my wife, Margaret, who is also called Rushes Bear. For the spirits, again, have called on her. Let us speak of her vision.

"This vision occurred to Margaret in the bush where the trees grow thick, near our cabin. That is when she saw the making of this dress, which some of you know was made with nothing ever touched by the chimookomaanag. This dress is sacred. This dress was made with healing in mind. So how, you wonder, did old Nanapush come to wear it?

"That is a very good question.

"Some of you are my friends, and some of you are my enemies. I make no distinction, but tell the truth no matter who you are. Whether you love me or hate me does not affect my story. Although I have faith in the old ways, I finally was persuaded to try the Eucharist last night. Father Damien and my dear wife have been after me for years to receive the benefit of the whiteman's God, and at last, I did give in to their wishes. In one night, I made up for all of the years of the blood of Christ that I had missed. I drank a whole keg. Inspired by the sacramental wine, and perhaps a little mad, I persuaded my wife to let me wear her holy dress. In her compassion for me, she gave it up, saying that it contained a powerful medicine that might work with the wine to give me insight and wisdom into the grave problem now before us.

"I am not afraid, as others may be, that my manhood will be compromised by such a little thing as wearing a skirt. My manhood is made of stiffer stuff. No, I was not concerned for that. Rather, I worried that I, like so many other men who boast of their superiority and revel in their brute strength, cleverness, or power, was unworthy to wear the dress of a woman."

Here I paused. I took a close look at my crowd. My initial impression—that it was composed of two women to every one man—was confirmed. I went on.

"We call the earth Grandmother. We ask her help when times are difficult. When we are lonely, or harrowed by death, we throw ourselves upon her and weep onto her breast. All that we are and all that we survive upon comes from the Grandmother. There is nothing she does not provide. But there is a limit to everything, even your grandma's patience. How many of you have had a spoon thrown at your head? When I donned my wife's dress, I admit that I was at first defiant and, as I have confessed to you, quite drunk. But the dress itself is sacred as you know, and even though I am a clever fool it stopped my thoughts and humbled me and made me listen.

"It wasn't that the dress spoke to me. It was that my ears were opened to hear all I missed when I was arrayed like a man.

"Listen, old fool, I heard the earth tell me. You are walking on my beautiful body. And I allow it—not because you are a human and not because you are a man—but because you were born of a woman. I, the earth, respect a woman's pain as it is freely given to the service of life. The only time you men suffer is when your bellies are stretched too full from the food your wives cook for you. Hear me out, you poor, split creature! Poor man, decorated with a knob and a couple of balls! You're only here on my patience and on the patience of women. What would you do, the earth asked me laughingly, if all women of the world closed their legs to men? Die out, that's what. So with my generous nature. I have given you all that you have. You owe your life to me.

"Now I ask you, what have you given to me in return?"

I turned to my relatives, my people, and opened my arms wide.

"What have we given her?" To my question, there was no answer. I'd said enough. I walked off and left the assembly to ponder my words. When they voted, they rejected the land settlement. So the dress worked. The medicine was the sacred shame that it provoked in me. I was humbled, and in that mood I decided to return to Margaret. As I neared the cabin, I began an anxious series of requests, all based on my love of Margaret. I hoped she would greet me, no matter how angry. I would endure her whipping tongue, bear the bite of her disdain, if only she would be there, I thought, waiting for me whether to kiss or kill. But when I got to our little home the door was shut, the cabin empty, the stove cold, and her blanket gone. I stood in the center of the quiet, sick and wondering.

What gives us such cause to harm each other? Where do we come by the substance of our anger and pride? I had no doubt even then that Margaret loved me and I loved her. Yet as a couple our main activity, it seemed, was making each other miserable.

"Please come home," I cried out the open door, into the bush, "and let me love you the way you deserve!"

But from the massed green leaves and the thick growing trees, there was no answer, nor from the weedy flowers or the berries or the silence of the birds. At that moment, I understood that the manidoog were tired of me, too, that I'd gone one step too far. I sank to the earth, put my head in my hands. With all my heart I wished to be forgiven. Going back through the nights and days I began to count up all I'd done to the people around me and chance passersby too. I tried to name each name, I tried to beg their mercy and humbly address each problem I'd created starting with the day I tried to snare Shesheeb. I began with good intentions, but I quickly fell asleep. The list was too long. The day too warm. The breeze so calm and golden.

TWELVE

The Fortune

Polly Elizabeth

*T*HERE WAS NO packing of the house, since its entire contents would be sold at auction. John James Mauser had fled, leaving me to clean up the copious mess of his belongings, but it was after all part of the agreement. He was to wander the earth. I was to count his handkerchiefs. After I had totaled them up I was to then mark them with a price. I would handle the sale of his accumulated goods, and with the proceeds I would satisfy as many of his creditors as I possibly could. Fleur had taken the automobile, her clothing, and the boy. They had departed before dawn and would take back roads in case they should be followed by those who were alerted to the entire desertion of John James Mauser—the abandonment of his ruined accounts and the bled carcasses of his books and the plucked spars of the solid edifice that once had been his moneyed life.

And here I was, counting handkerchiefs. To add strangeness to surprise, I was not alone. I was joined. He was polishing a table spread with silver. He had brown eyes and a smile that I now saw as one of unbounded attraction, for it was cast upon me out of love. When Fantan looked at me, the sun came out in any room, and when I looked back at him, I could feel soft fire rise in my own face. What astounding things can happen to us, what change, what absurd luck.

We've lost a fortune, for Mauser's money of course was the stipend upon which my sister and I lived. But I have gained more than a fortune. I have Fantan. We have plans, grand plans. We are heading north to live in a town just outside the reservation boundary. A little place with a railroad spur and two bars, a piano shop, a newspaper, and a grain elevator. Fantan has saved a small bundle of money, and Mauser secretly added to it before he was picked clean. With it we've bought a share in a trading store located on the reservation. Eventually we'll buy out the half still belonging to the old Lebanese, and then we'll move into the store's back rooms. We will live at the ends of the earth. We will sell dried peas and shovels. Fabric and spools of thread. I'll train a bean vine around the back door and I'll have a garden filled with squash. Fantan will play cards with Fleur as often as he can, and I'll read sweet poems to the boy, no matter how big he grows.

Fantan touches my shoulder and my arm glows. My hand is in his hand. With our box of pens and tags, we're moving on to the bedside clocks. The racks of ties. The unwrapped boxes of cigars.

All that Mauser left. Wherever I go in the house, now, Fantan is at my side and the little dog follows us both. I look down at my black Diablo, head on his paws. He is at my feet. He knows that he must trust to my forgiveness for his daily meat. So he wags his plumed tail and noses at my foot and I pat him gently. Affection, I tell him, is how a dog survives. Knowing how to exist without it is how a woman wrests her life into her own hands. But then it comes, it takes one by surprise. Affection and freedom and the will to risk. Everything that happened since I answered the door to Fleur was leading up to this. Warm sun falls on us through diamonds of lead glass as we work. If I am a fool, I am proud to be one. I have married one servant and declared another my sister. My husband and I do not speak in flows of words, but we connect by the heartstrings and by laughter and by signs. I am that rare thing thought only to exist in death. I am a happy woman.

THIRTEEN

Red Jacket Beans

Nanapush

WHEN I WOKE on the false
floor that Margaret had traded away for most of her son's
birthright land, I swam for a while in the world of my dreams.
There was my gentle Omiimii, the touch of her hand soft as air.
There was my comical Red Cradle, licking maple sugar. As dawn
came, I saw my father walking over the hill into a great band of
brilliance. Then all but his shadow was consumed by light. I rose,
drank gallons of water from the pump we were so fortunate to
have, then realized I was still wearing Margaret's dress. I took it
off. The hem was ripped here and there, but repairable I thought.
I would sew it. Naked, I lay in the sun and gathered my strength

to ply the needle. Once I felt stronger, I rose and searched for my clothing, but couldn't find my pants, at least in one piece.

Ai! My woman had revenged herself! For there they were, my pants, all ripped to pieces scattered here and there upon the floor. My woman challenges me, I muttered out loud. Fair enough! Inside of her sewing box there was a needle, thread, and sinew. I would not only repair her dress, but I would splice my shreds of pants back together. I knew very well that for me to be seen with her in such raggedy pants (perhaps next Sunday at Holy Mass, no matter how hard she banged her stick) would be infinitely more humiliating to Margaret than if I showed up naked.

I sat on a folded blanket and began the tedious process of piecing together my trousers. What I made was soon composed more of holes and thread than any cloth. Margaret had been most thorough in her destruction. Some pieces were the size of chokecherry leaves and others were not only tiny but bitten or chewed up into the bargain, as if she'd vented her rage by gnashing the cloth between her teeth. Evidence of such a fabulous fury should have been enough to warn me off the whole enterprise. Or at least I should have gone somewhere else in my thoughts and fears. Not to the same old place I'd been for so long—back to Shesheeb. But here's a human truth that cannot be denied, no matter how painful: Jealousy is a powerful, many-toothed creature whose bite leaves a poison in the blood. I was not rid of all that poison yet. It was with me, affecting my brain.

I fell to brooding. Each little piece of maliciousness, each wounding word, each cruel joke between myself and Margaret made its way back to pain me anew. Each time I remembered some bitter exchange, the various emotions that went along with it boiled up inside me like a foul sap. I could not help dwelling especially on the most recent things she had said about Shesheeb, the searing compliments. The boasts of his riches and cleverness. His knowledge of old-time medicines. His powers. So he could change into a fly! I laughed out loud, my voice scratchy from last night's singing. Very appropriate. He was a maggot in his youth. Flies fed on shit. If he showed up in such a form I'd swat him dead.

"I invite you," I muttered. "I dare you. I would enjoy it!" I wasn't serious of course, just thinking aloud. Nevertheless, as though in answer to my speech, a fat, black, buzzing blowfly, just the sort of fly that Shesheeb would be if he turned himself into a fly, landed on the sorry old crust of bannock I was about to eat, and began cleaning off its legs.

I took the floppy makizin off my foot and hit, missed the fly, sent my bannock spinning across the slippery linoleum floor. The fat thing lifted off and began to buzz just out of reach. When you're nursing a vengeful hangover, there is nothing more irritating than a fly, not to mention a big one with a loud gassy sputter that insists on dive-bombing your swollen, aching head. Again and again it attacked, brushing my ear, my neck. I could not destroy the thing. I tried, but could not connect. Its clever persistence infuriated me. I stalked the fly, tried to sneak up on it, swatted dozens of times, and always missed. I sat very still beside a spot of syrup I used as bait. Poised with my makizin ready to hit it. But time and time again, it disregarded the sticky syrup, landed on the makizin and then bumbled off with a mocking clatter of its dirty wings. The fly laughed at me by sitting still, then disappearing when I moved. It anticipated where my shoe would land. I was halfway across the room only to have it buzz my head. I began to think that it was more than a fly. It read my mind. It played with me, flashing beneath my nose and then vanishing, until finally I lost all patience and uttered a murderous howl that raised the bark off the trees.

"Shesheeb," I screamed, and leaped after the fly, batting right and left, destroying the careful arrangement of Margaret's house. Wild to kill, I tipped over baskets, burst bags, capsized her stacked tins. Flour sifted through the air. Coffee burst out upon the floor. Margaret's carefully sorted beads spilled crazily across the linoleum. Her bundles of herbs spun off the wall. Still, I could not kill the fly.

"I give up." I collapsed finally. "I hope I wounded the old bugger, or at least showed him I meant business." For a moment, there was utter calm. The cabin was still. I got to my feet hoping the war was finished, but then the fly buzzed me, brushing my face with its filthy wings.

I snapped, then, like a stick that can only stand so much bending. I threw myself down and held the tender bag of my throbbing head. It was from that depth that I was visited by a most private urge. My ojiid called out sternly for attention, for release. It was then, in a state of sorry derangement, abandoned by the love of my life, hung over, tormented by a fly, that I sank to a new low of cunning.

"Hey, Shesheeb," I cried, "ombay omah." I pulled down my pants and let go right on the floor. In moments, the foul bug landed on what I left. In one swift move, I clapped a lard pail over it. Silence. Triumph, of sorts. Either I had bested Shesheeb, at last, or captured my own shit. Now what? Bury it, lard pail and all, I told myself. So I went outside and grimly dug a hole in the corner of the clearing. Returning, I tapped on the pail. An annoyed buzz answered from within. How to make certain of my little captive? Ah! I had knocked to the floor our sharpest skinning knife. Retrieving it, I plunged it into the linoleum and carefully cut a circle out around the can. Then securing the can, fly, and moowan, I carried the whole thing outside most carefully and with utmost precision buried it in the ground.

After I had tamped down the earth and smoothed it over, I came back to my senses. I still had not succeeded in repairing my pants or Margaret's dress. Instead, I had given myself a whole new problem. I walked back into the cabin. There, in the center of Margaret's greatest pride, her linoleum, was the hole I'd confidently cut around the lard can. Margaret would be more than furious—she would never forgive me in this life, or the next life. I was doomed to a lonely outcast's death forever, unless I could come up with an explanation.

I put my mind to it. Marshaled my sagging wit, my faltering brain. The afternoon shadows crept out and I feared that now Margaret would make her way home. I thought of darkness. The moon at half. Stars. Something about the thought of stars hung me up, maybe something I could pin my survival on. I focused on those stars. As I did, one fell out of the sky in a lingering arc of fire, and I suddenly knew the answer.

In a fever, I calculated the exact place on the roof that the hole would have to be cut for the star to have blasted through, and blazed on to destroy Margaret's floor. Quickly, as the shadows ran into one another, blending into darkness, I worked. I burned the edges of the hole in the floor, then I went on top of the roof, cut the corresponding hole and scorched its edges, too. When I

167

was finished, the burnt and ragged holes matched precisely. Then I rehearsed. I would tell Margaret that I was minding my own damn business and sleeping when out of the heavens that star sizzled down right through the roof and went through the floor too and made that regrettable hole. It was unfortunate—here I practiced my sorrowful look—but exciting at the same time. A blazing, shooting star! As I practiced my story, elaborating on the sight, I thrilled myself. What a marvel! The hole in our roof was not just any hole, nor was the hole in the floor. They were evidence of a celestial event, a proof of something essential and special—perhaps that Margaret and I were meant for each other. I looked from the hole in the ceiling to the floor and back again. Troubled, suddenly, I stared at the hole in the floor through which there was visible a patch of the earth beneath the house. For now the hole raised yet another question. Where was the star itself? It would have buried itself in the earth beneath the house. Margaret, no fool, would surely dig to find it. Of what does a star consist? What does a star look like once it reaches the earth?

WHEN THE original fire tore itself ragged out of the sky and plunged to earth, only scraps of it, the stars, were left. We were all made of that original fire. The stars are relatives. Yet we have no idea how they appear up close, and that was my problem. Questions upon questions I had never thought to ask. If stars are fire, upon what substance does their burning feed? Is there a core, something visible? How are these fires fixed and supplied? Most important, how much of this did Margaret know, and what would persuade her that one had fallen through the roof?

There were of course the Catholic stars painted on the ceiling of the church—these were guided by a far simpler history. Gilded by Father Damien's wish and desire, they gleamed in a false sky. Five-pointed and of a regular decorative shape, they were easy to mimic. In the end, I couldn't think of any other solution but that my star would be a Catholic star. I couldn't pluck one off the vault of the church, though, and would have to find some other source.

I thought of chipping one from stone and dipping it in golden paint that I would beg from Father Damien, but when I considered the entire procedure I knew I hadn't the time. I thought of carving a star of wood, but Margaret might consider it odd that the star hadn't burnt itself up. And how would a tree grow far off in the sky, anyway, and who would have carved such a thing but me? No, the answer lay somewhere else. Metal, I thought, would be perfect. I picked up Margaret's baking pan and wished that I could think of a way she wouldn't miss it. I could cut the star from the pan with a very sharp knife, but she knew every dent in its surface, every scar, every nick. She would immediately catch on to me and then on top of her roof and her linoleum I would have destroyed her pan. No. There must be something else. And sure enough. Once I examined with a purposeful eye each object in our cabin, the answer jumped out at me. The humble bean can. There it sat, emptied of its beans in making the rabbit stew I had absurdly rejected. Used ever since then for nothing but skimming, it contained only a bit of venison fat that Margaret surely wouldn't miss.

I cleaned the can out and removed the label, to be burnt. I polished the can until the metal shone, studied it for inspiration on where to make my cuts. Down the sides, I decided, and the bottom would be the center of the star. I then proceeded, using infinitesimal care. Cutting slowly, shielding my fingers from the sharp edges with a bit of moosehide, I made what turned out to be a spectacular star. Using careful diagonal cuts along each ray, I curled the edges with a spoon's side and a dull knife. It was a picture. Ojibwe ingenuity knows no limits, I congratulated myself. Better than I'd dared to hope, the star was strange, rich, and complicated. I had never seen a thing like it. I could sure not tell it had ever been a lowly tin can.

"You will save my hide," I said to my creation, turning it this way and that to catch the light. I proceeded to dig a space directly beneath the hole in the linoleum and to bury the star in the dirt, right where I'd say it fizzled out.

WHEN MARGARET returned to the cabin, I had planned to be lying out cold on the floor next to the hole, or staring at the hole with a gaping mouth, as though dazzled by the catastrophe. But she caught me by surprise. She was so long in showing up that I ate the rest of a wheel of bannock she'd forgotten, and fell asleep on the sagging pole bed in the corner.

"Gitimishk!" she cried, finding me there.

I was chagrined to be found and called lazy. I rubbed my eyes, and quickly remembered my plan. I must present myself as addled and confused by the star's blazing passage. I blinked and squinted, pretending to try to focus on her.

"How the light hurts my eyes," I complained.

"What light?"

"The fire!" I roared suddenly as though in fear. She looked around in irritation, taking in the mess, and it was then she saw the hole in the floor, a dark and gaping spot, jagged around the edges. It looked to be still smoldering. It was even uglier and stranger to one who chanced upon it, and Margaret gasped in horror to behold the destruction. Speechless in shock, she turned to me. And I was ready with the story, completely prepared to act the part. In my excitement, I almost persuaded myself. I showed her exactly how close I was standing when the star blasted through the roof, leaving the hole through which a sweetly clouded sky was now visible. With my hands, swooping in a swift movement, I indicated the star's trajectory. I showed her how far I'd leaped for safety, and then I displayed the pan of water I had poured from the storage can to douse the bits of fire that trailed in the star's wake. Margaret nodded, her mouth open, astonished at the strangeness of my story, but nearly convinced. Encouraged, I invented the extraordinary scorching sensations I had suffered as the hot star plunged itself into our floor. It occurred to me to add how close I'd come to being struck and killed. A bit more to one side or the other and she would have found her love, her only Nanapush, a smoldering heap. Silence fell after that as she stared at me, sinking toward me in contemplation of her close call with loss. A look of forgiving softness, a tender blossoming of sentiment warred with her wrath at the ruin of her linoleum. Forgiveness began in her, I could tell by the slight tremor at one edge of her lower lip, but she caught it with her sharp tooth. Her eyes were still suspicious.

"And this star," she reasoned, just as I had anticipated, "after it burned through my beautiful floor, destroying my floor, it must have extinguished its light in the dirt."

"Mii nange," I said, "of course! Unless it burned itself deep into earth, beyond reach, it is surely there."

Margaret fixed me with a challenging look in which there was a hint of an ironic smile, and I saw that I hadn't quite managed to persuade her of my story. This would be the test. She waited for me to offer to dig, and when I made no move she gave a slightly contemptuous snort and fetched her heavy cook spoon, her good steel one. That she would use her precious spoon to dig dirt impressed me with the serious nature of her cause and I inwardly congratulated myself on thinking past her, on creating the star, on burying it in the precise spot where she was digging now. Even more so, the minute she found it, did I inwardly rejoice. For once the earth was brushed off my creation's points and curlicues, how it gleamed and caught the light! Margaret held the star out in amazement and turned it around in her hands. I watched her face as the knowledge of the vastness of her find sank in. She was absorbing this, I could see it, she was filling with belief. She was imagining herself the owner of this visitor from the sky world, or from the whiteman's heaven. She was picturing the many curious visits and questions from relatives and friends. She was even forming in her mind the story I had given, which would become her story too. For a long while, she stared in wonder at the star. Then carried it in two hands, carefully, to the table beside our window.

"Old man," she said, very softly at last, "I believe we have been chosen for some purpose. First the medicine dress. Now this!"

"Yes, my sweet face," I gravely agreed with her, barely containing the force of my delight, "we must have been chosen."

From outside, the sun, striking sudden from behind a cloud, then threw a fierce shaft of light in our direction. It slanted through the window and picked out the star in Margaret's hands. Marveling at it, she bent to examine it with a close eye. I smiled to see her, but the smile dropped off my face when with a huge gasp she squinted even closer and then slowly, slowly, with a dangerously changed expression held her miraculous find out to me.

"Put on your spectacles, old liar," she said in a softly charged voice.

Immediately, I hooked them around my ears and in the burst of radiance I saw the raised letters I had missed in the tin, now the center of the star, which had marked the bottom of the can. Red Jacket Beans. I lifted my eyes to hers with the hopeless shame and contrition of a dog caught halfway in the stew pot. Nothing would get me out of this now. She glared back at me and for a long time our gazes held over my bean-can star. I saw something building in her, something gathering, a storm, and my heart sank down into my feet. But when it came, it was not the bitter scorching, not the fire I feared. It was not the horror of sarcasm. Not the scrape of reproach. Margaret did something she had never done before in response to one of my idiot transgressions. Margaret laughed.

FOURTEEN

The Medicine Dress

Margaret

*A*s THE SNARE my old man had
set tightened around my neck, I felt my life squeezing out. A haze
of yellow spots covered up my vision, but I wasn't gone yet, for
through that awful radiance I saw the dress. Transparent at first,
then made of impossible materials. Even though my life ebbed, I
couldn't help planning. Wondering. How do you make a dress of
water? How do you make a dress of fish scales and blood? A dress
of stone? I saw a dress of starvation worn meager. I saw an assim-
ilation dress of net and foam. A communion dress worn by my
mother, who tried to live white and then abandoned her attempt.
I saw a dress made of bear's breath. A dress of lake weed and fury.
A dress of whiskey. A dress of loss. I had been working on that

dress all my life. The noose jerked. My heart cracked. I was filled with a terrible sorrow to know that I would not be able to finish that healing garment.

Then the fool man saved me, or so it seemed, but really, I knew it was the dress wanting to be sewed.

To sew is to pray. Men don't understand this. They see the whole but they don't see the stitches. They don't see the speech of the creator in the work of the needle. We mend. We women turn things inside out and set things right. We salvage what we can of human garments and piece the rest into blankets. Sometimes our stitches stutter and slow. Only a woman's eye can tell. Other times, the tension in the stitches might be too tight because of tears, but only we know what emotion went into the making. Only women can hear the prayer.

So the medicine dress wanted me to make it. A privilege I might have had no use for twenty years ago. Or forty. But now that I have lived upon this earth and seen what I have seen, I was ready. And so I began where all things begin—with the death of something else.

The power of the dress lay in the strict rules of its making, so I got my boys to drive a young cow moose into the water, then they roped and knocked her out while she was swimming across the lake. They killed her without the use of any whiteman's weapon, and dragged her in by hand, lay spent on shore marveling at how the old-timers managed to do these things. Meanwhile, I went to work. To skin the moose, I used an ancient chipped spear point I had found one day while digging my squash vines under. The edge was still sharp, but I ground it sharper on a flint. It took me a good, long, bloody while to skin the moose, but I did it. When I was finished, I distributed the meat and took the hides. Removed the brain

to tan the hides. Soaked the hides in ashes and water, then carried them dripping to the log bench I set up behind the cabin. I
began rolling the hide, scraping it with the shoulder blade, pulling
it across that log, manhandling it all one day and the next day, until
I got it where I wanted it. Softer than chimookomaan velvet, softer
than a hopeless touch, strong and long wearing but open to the
needle. Which I made from a fish bone. I smoked that hide butter-
brown and then I sat down to begin. I figured how the hides would
cover me and talked as I sewed. Told the dress things I hadn't
remembered for fifty years.

I told the dress all about who I was as a child. You wouldn't
think it to look at me now, I said, but I was not only very pretty but
stronger than all of the boys. My mother hid me from the agents
at the government school for as long as she could. Where did she
hide me? A place they would never look. Under my great-grandmother's skirt, behind the two stony posts of her legs. She was so
old that she could not be moved from the corner of the cabin. All
day, she sat on her little wooden chair with the curved back. Her
mouth moved and her blind white eyes flickered. She chewed willow bark tobacco, and sucked constantly on chokecherry pits.
Sometimes she passed me down a strip of jerky, where I hid underneath a balloon of calico broadcloth, a tent that smelled of sweet
grass and stale piss, of potato-cellar dust and crushed mint pillows,
of smoked moosehide, safe. School agents tramped around looking for me. Kookum closed her eyes and snored. When they awak-
ened her, she screamed louder than a magpie, began to snarl,
clawed the air until they retreated from the cabin in alarm.

"There, my girl," she would say, patting my head. "Now you
are safe for another year. Did you see something under my dress?"

"Oh no, kookum," I would tell her. I would call her Gitchinookomis. I would offer her respectful thanks. But in truth I had seen something as I looked out from under her leg posts, from my place underneath her where it was darker than darkness. That something was not anything my husband's dirty mind would invent. I'd seen something else, invisible and sacred. Time opened for me. I saw back through my gitchi-nookomisiban to the woman before, her mother, and the woman before that, who bore her, and the woman before that, too. All of those women had walked carefully upon this earth, I knew, otherwise they would not have survived. I saw back through a woman named Standing Strong to her mother named Fish Bones to her mother named Different Thunder. Yellow Straps. Sky Coming Down. Lightning Proof (Gitchi-nookomisiban told me she was struck and lived, but people next to her were sometimes scorched). I sat with my great-grandmother every night after that. She was my school. She told me all about the women reaching back into the darkness. How people always avoided Steps Over Truth when they wanted a straight answer, and I Hear when they wanted to keep a secret. As for Glittering, she put soot on her face and watched for enemies at night. The woman named Standing Across could see things moving far across the lake. The old ladies gossiped about Playing Around, but no one dared say anything to her face. Ice was good at gambling. Shining One Side loved to sit and talk to Opposite the Sky. Rabbit, Prairie Chicken, and Daylight were all friends of Gitchi-nookomisiban when they were little girls. She Tramp could make great distance in a day of walking. Cross Lightning had a powerful smile. When Setting Wind and Gentle Woman Standing sang together, the whole tribe listened. Stop the Day got her name when at her shout the afternoon went still. Log was strong, great-grandmother remembered, Cloud Touching Bottom was weak and consumptive. Mirage married Wind, and then married everyone. Children loved Musical Cloud, but hid from Dressed in Stone. Lying Down Grass had such a gentle voice and touch, but no one dared to cross She Black of Heart.

After the priests came among us, my great-grandmother said, She Knows the Bear became Marie. Sloping Cloud was christened Jeanne. Taking Care of the Day and Yellow Day Woman turned into Catherines. I became Margaret, but I always knew that would happen. The year they carried my great-grandmother out the western window, wrapped in red cloth and then tied into birch bark, the school finally got me. The girl who was named Center of the Sky became Margaret, then Margaret Kashpaw and then Rushes Bear. But I had already seen far back in time by then. I knew who I was in relation to all who went before. Therefore, although I went to school I was not harmed, nor while I was there did I forget my language. Not Margaret. Every time I was struck or shamed for speaking Ojibwemowin, I said to myself, *There's another word I won't forget.* I tamped it down. I took it in. I grew hard inside so that the girl named Center of the Sky could survive. Some think that I am mean, but that is why I'm with the living yet. My husband outwitted death by talking. So did I. Only when his talk was comical, kind, and obscene, mine was cutting and angry. I've been that way. The dress may change me. Or my talking to it, much the same.

I told the dress about my vision and I skipped stones across the water of my life, described the sensation of having my head shaved by those Lazarres. I told my dress about the distinctive ways each of my babies was born—what they looked like the first time I saw them and how they grew. Where they were now—scattered to the four directions of the earth. I told the medicine dress about Nector and Eli, my so-called twins, and their miserable mistakes with women. I trusted the dress and told it about the loss of my beauty, how difficult that was for a woman who used to rely upon it. Finally, I told the dress about Nanapush, or attempted to give some idea of all he is capable of doing and thinking. I didn't get far. Nanapush is the only man I've never seen entirely through, never thoroughly understood. He has loved me with all his foolish heart, which at first outraged me. But for a long time now, secretly, I've let myself be charmed. I told the dress that I would die with him although he is an imbecile.

NANAPUSH collected the bones of the birds I required to decorate the dress, and he roamed the bush for the roots and stems I used for dye. I cut the bones into bead lengths and made a yoke of plum, rose, softest yellow. I used red willow and chokecherry bark to dye the quills and I wove them into the dress, thinking how my words stabbed, like those quills, when my husbands got too near me. When a quill sinks in deep, there is a barb in the tip that anchors the quill so it will work its way in ever deeper, to fester and kill. Only by clipping off the end of the quill and puffing air through the hollow can the barb safely be released. I'd done it many times with a snout-poked animosh. Perhaps, I thought, I'd buried my quills too deeply by now in my last husband's heart. The poison might have lain there too long. Things might be too far gone. I couldn't tell. But as I worked on the dress, it seemed to work on me. I was surprised to find that when I thought back to the snare that nearly killed me, I didn't blame Nanapush. Not in my heart. I know I had purposely quickened his jealousy, and for no reason. Like a young girl who doesn't know any better, I was taunting him, playing with his love, twisting up the sinews of his poor old heart.

Enough, I told myself. Mi'iw. Enough.

Even when he rolled back to the cabin, drunk as the keg itself, I wasn't angry. I never laid into him. In fact, it crossed my mind to lay otherwise, even though the old man reeked. I nearly brought him to bed. I might have. I had it in my mind. If only his arrogant ways had not surfaced, if only he hadn't challenged me to let him dance in my dress. Sometimes, if all my patience has had no effect, my anger gets twice the better of me. So it was, I left my old man wearing the medicine dress, and started out for Shesheeb's house. Driven to it! I told myself. Forced into the arms of someone I hated, from the arms of the man I loved!

I am too old for such dramas to be played out upon my body. For a long time now, I've let myself slide toward comfortable ruin without even pretending concern. Loved by Nanapush, I had a wealth that I could squander. His love oppressed me at times, but I also valued it. As I walked through the bush, I smiled to recall the absurd sight the old man cut, dancing in my dress. Rather than afflict me with fury, it made me laugh. Which is why, as I made my way through the diamond willow and around the deep slough and over the little crossing to the house of Shesheeb, even then, I knew I was bluffing. I had no wish for troubles of the heart. No wish to take revenge on my childish husband. Revenge was beneath the stature I'd found as a woman. I reached the clearing in which the old duck's house was set, and I even sat down on a little stump at the edge and had a smoke of my pipe, which I carried with me in a pouch that hung off my belt. After a while, I saw Shesheeb come out into the yard. He poked around, stopped to scratch his old duck's balls, and generally made himself such an unattractive prospect that I melted away from the scene.

TO LOVE Nanapush, to love at all, is like trying to remember the tune and words to a song that the spirits have given you in your sleep. Some days, I knew exactly how the song went and some days I couldn't even hum the first line. Then there were times we both knew the song and love was effortless. Our old years flowed along, carrying us quickly in a rush. At least we were together, if at odds. No matter how foolishly my husband behaved, no matter how dreadful his mistakes, jokes, and sins, he loved me. In that, my suspicious woman's heart came to trust. Somehow, between the exhaustion leveled on me by all previous men and the steady, if crazy, love-fortitude of this one, the good days came closer together for the two of us. I numbered the days on one hand and was nearly at the end of the years on the other—our lives had progressed that far—when it happened. As we always knew, as we had waited for, as was inevitable, Fleur returned.

SHE CAME BACK so rich that we didn't know, at first, whether the slim woman in the white car, and the whiter suit fitted to the lean contours of her body, was the ghost of the girl we knew or Fleur herself. It was a dry afternoon. The dust swirled in a tan gray cloud when she stopped. Slowly, as she got out and stood beside the car, the dust settled around her feet like a dropped cape. She was left in the clear air, staring hard at the steps of the trader's store, where I stood. When she saw me, her eye lit and she smiled—that direct punishment that men take for invitation.

Only to me it was this: acknowledgment. It was as though she and I had known this from the very beginning. It would come down to us in spite of all the men's doings—us two women.

Then I noticed the pale blur of a face in the window of the car, and he stepped out, too, shaking his fat legs, frowning. This last time she left the reservation and returned, Fleur Pillager brought back a son. Not that we understood, at first, the connection. He seemed too soft, too baby fine, too chubby, too white, to be any son of Fleur Pillager's, so at first gossip had it the boy was stolen goods. Kidnapped. Taken from whatever too-fine place he was spawned in return for the child Fleur had lost so long ago. The mean and envious waited, all eager, for her arrest. That never happened. The boy was big and hulking, his face was round, anxious, shut. He had not one of his mother's features and he was spoiled. A pouter, he'd have his way or sulk for candy. We watched as he took big bites, filled his face with sweet sugar, powdery cakes, and was always seen with a bulging pocket eyeing other children with piggy suspicion.

As soon as I saw the boy, I put his presence together with what I knew of Lulu's hatred of her mother. The story was not hard to assemble. In sorrow over losing Lulu and the tiny one besides, Fleur had warped this one. Kept him too close, plied him, spoiled him, sweeted him. None of which would have made the slightest difference to a child of strong, raw stuff. But it was clear to see that from the beginning this one was liquid dough, half baked, demanding, and full of longing. There was also damage in him not of Fleur's own making.

Perhaps the Pillager stuff was all used up in Fleur. She was the last, and like the longest-boiled kettle of maple sap, she was the strongest and darkest. Or if the Pillager stuff had not given out, maybe it was blocked. Perhaps the spirits of all those she had sent on the death road had lined up against her on the other side. I pictured it. Drowned men glared into her cabin with dead, white eyes. Frozen men, their hair drifted over with crystals of ice, stared at her star-lashed in hollow unforgiveness. The one in the lake was jealous. My own son, Eli, would never be the same after knowing Fleur Pillager. He lived alone in the woods with only spirits for company. Had he cursed her? Had all of them? Why had she no children who'd call her mother? And now, this boy.

I took the woods trail back to the house, in order to consider things. Fleur took the roads. She was there when I arrived. Her white car was parked between the lines of pink stones. I stood half hidden, watching her remove the bones and the markers and the cloth from the trunk of her car, and pile them in the middle of a split birch. As I walked to the door, I remembered how years ago Fleur had shaved her own head to halve my shame, and the thought of us two, heads gleaming like dark, peeled onions, made me laugh. I was eager to hold her close and wished as I always did that love had worked out between Fleur and Eli. I couldn't help it. Fleur Pillager was the daughter of my spirit.

She met me halfway there. She held my arms and smiled at me and I knew it. I saw it right then plain as plain. Her spirit was still longing for her old place, her land, her scraped-bare home that had nothing on it but kind popple, raspberry bushes, and a cabin caved in from last year's snow.

FIFTEEN

The Game of Nothing

Nanapush

*T*HE AGENCY DOORS shut behind Fleur Pillager, and she and Bernadette Morrissey were together in the land office. Those who happened to be passing by the agency turned on their heels and happened to pass back. Those who'd followed Fleur stopped and waited inside the shadow of the building, and those who'd tried to stop her—that is, Margaret and myself—sat on the agency steps. Fleur's son sat next to me, whittling away at a splinter that had once been a thick knot of wood. We waited, breathless, as though we'd hear what was going on behind those walls. But all that happened was Fleur came out of the door. Then got into the car with her boy and drove off. We felt cheated of entertainment; all the same we were relieved.

The second time she walked into the agency office fewer stood by, and fewer yet the third time and the fourth. It became accepted and then barely noticed. It was part of the day and people got used to seeing her come or go. Still, no one knew what she did once inside the office. And nobody but me seemed to wonder why it should be the same repeat visit at the same time of the day every day. It didn't take me long to recognize Fleur's poker game, the one she had played for Argus men's wages, where she raked them in slow with a hunter's patience and then sprang her trap. Routine was her favorite strategy. Odd, annoying, humble. And dangerous. The next day, I followed her through the doorway and stood behind her. Fleur was dressed in the same white suit she'd worn when she first appeared on the reservation. The fabric was unmarred. The suit's lines were the same, stiff and elegant. The cuffs and collar and lapel were made of a material woven with thin, black stripes, so a person had to get up close to detect the slightest hint that the suit had been worn all week. Oh, and the hat. A small black-and-white peaked hat sewn with a clever brim and a spotted veil. At first Fleur had worn it with her hair pinned strictly into a suave roll. For the last two days, ominously perhaps, she had let down her hair and divided it into braids. So her appearance, as I stood behind her, was oddly disconnected, the braids sinuous and shining against the haughty pinch-waisted figure she cut in that suit. She asked one question.

"Have you found out?"

Once she had the answer, always negative, she turned to go.

So I saw it then as I followed her back out into sunlight. Fleur had a question that Bernadette could answer but wouldn't, and in order to get the answer Fleur was engaged in what the Pillagers always did so well. Nothing. Perhaps, come to think of it, I might have taught this strategy to her myself. For the doing of nothing can be done in a certain way that makes the not-doing in itself an unnerving occurrence. That she would come into the agency every day wearing a suit the likes of which had not been worn hundreds of miles in any direction from where she stood, that she would ask her question every day and not cease or do anything else until it was answered, was clear. That she would be calm, that she would be patient and implacable, was also a given. I enjoyed having Fleur to watch and so did everyone else, except Bernadette, who was shortly exposed as either hiding the answer or not knowing it, for of course once I followed Fleur other people did too, in order to hear the question, the same as always, and the answer that eventually changed from no to the name Jewett Parker Tatro.

He owned Fleur's land now. From what I can construct of the ownership history, Fleur had brought the deed back to the reservation signed to her in Mauser's hand and witnessed, only to be told that Mauser had taken his turn after her in not paying his taxes. By plaguing Bernadette, she found that the taxes were paid and the land was bought from the state by Jewett Tatro. He was white and an Indian agent to boot, or a former one. He was now the owner of a bar that he called the Wild Goose. He should not have been allowed to buy reservation land at all, but there was a loophole year, during which the state government had passed a bill that allowed such transfers. The bill was found to contradict federal law and so was nullified, but not quickly enough to prevent Tatro's smooth theft. And the land once bought and lost from our tribal trust was not to be returned. It never is. *Don't let it go*, I tell the people. It never comes back. Unless someone like Fleur has lost the land and wants it returned and is willing and audacious, and again I say patient enough, adept enough at the doing of nothing, to set up a deadfall. A deadfall of boredom. Here is what happened. Shortly after she got her answer Fleur changed her visits, both in time and place. No longer did she come to town every bright morning; she waited until evening, although she wore the same suit.

Now I should make it clear that I don't know how Fleur kept her suit clean. For while all of this was going on, she was living in her car. Oh, it was a fancy car, yes, and the seats were no doubt comfortable, front and back, though neither she nor her son could stretch out. But it sure didn't have running water. The car was parked everywhere and nowhere. She refused to stay with Margaret and me, partly because she just wouldn't, and partly because Lulu told her to leave. Oh, not in so many words or even by looking crosswise or snapping her eyes at her. It was not that direct. It was Lulu's absence that gave her the clear message. The way she could never be found. Fleur was at the house every day, and Lulu too, but the girl had that sly Pillager pre-knowledge, or just heard the engine maybe, and disappeared every time and before we knew it into the woods.

Meanwhile, Fleur lived in that car, and as I said she lived everywhere. Perhaps she hoped that if she parked in the right spot her daughter would creep near and love her. Or maybe she knew how truly uneasy and disruptive her here-and-there life was making the people. For it was upsetting. Not to know the whereabouts of that most particular Pillager weighed on people's nerves and caused everyone to look over their shoulders and peer down roads constantly. Old ladies filed reports with one another of Fleur's sightings. Along with the old men they kept an invisible watch. They constructed a mental pattern of her travels—here, there, she could be anywhere. That was the thing. Anywhere, nowhere. That white car and that woman in the white suit. Driving the reservation roads slowly, hardly raising any dust, and never stopping. No one ever saw where she parked to sleep, if she slept, or knew where she went to gas up, or if her car, which began to be seen as a ghost-car, even required such a thing as ordinary fuel or maybe ran on owl's breath, dark air. They didn't like it—there was tension. Things changed from interesting to uneasy. Disturbance lay over us. We saw Fleur's car idling near Tatro's bar and we saw him see her, or rather, see her automobile. We saw his eyes fixed on that fancy white car. So get it over with! That's what the old man said, all the old men younger than I am. Do what you're doing and be done with it! Mi'iw!

Fleur wasn't done yet. No apologies. More reckoning was in order and of course she needed her land. Signed over, safe, and in her name. And until that happened, everybody had to contend with a restless spirit in a car that never collected dust crisscrossing the whole reservation day and night as if patrolling. Or maybe trolling would be more like it, because by now everyone wanted to bite. What was she going to do? When would her car actually stop and park on the gray weed-afflicted bareness glittering with crushed and broken glass that surrounded the bar that nobody called by Tatro's fanciful name but instead just ziiginigewigamig, the pouring house, or Tatro's. When would she stop there and when would she leave her shell of white metal and walk into the one room and sit down at the table in the corner where an endless, low-stakes poker game went on day and night, never ended and never finished, never changed except that players came and went and always were replaced but usually by family members who looked similar, so that the game itself had become the reservation's purgatory, where once a person entered there was no way out. Someone else in your family surely would lose the amount you had won, for instance, and must borrow your winnings to retrieve the loss. Then you would have to step back into the game to make sure you got your loan back. On it would go. By this intricate means there was a fixed and yet shifting amount of money that might be owned or owed but eventually went back into the game so that over the years the figures and the numbers hovered in the air like an abstract cloud.

I suppose Fleur's entrance brought things down to earth. She was not there to enter into the game of eternal subtractions and additions. She was there to throw the balance off. She was there to get what she wanted and once she did she wouldn't give it back. It wouldn't ever go back into the game. Tatro didn't know this. In fact, he didn't know what she wanted at all. For a man who had lived among us for thirty years he had not learned much, but that wasn't why he stayed, anyway, to learn anything or know anything or even acquire things, though he did, as by now our most beautiful and even sacred objects hung upon the walls of his bar. They were either won in the poker game or traded to him for hard liquor—fair and square, we could not dispute that. Yet many turned their backs away from the wall in order to drink. These things were watching. Our grandmothers' and our grandfathers' hands had made them. And no, they shouldn't have been traded, should not have been sold except perhaps to feed a person's children. There were cradle boards, tight beaded on velvet, that once held the drunks beneath them. There were gun belts and shoulder bags that only our head men used to carry. Makizinan, old-time buckskin dresses, intricately woven purses and sashes and carrying bags. There was even a drum. Each thing represented, then, a transaction, which is what held Tatro. He really didn't know why he stayed at all and in fact he constantly harped on it and made all sorts of plans to go back east. He didn't know that what held him was the pain itself. It had got into and afflicted him. It had seeped down upon him from his loaded walls. He could not do much, less and less, except pour liquor and play cards. On some days, he didn't get out of his bed and only dragged himself out when his all-night bartender threatened to quit unless he was relieved. Once he got his day started, Tatro usually revived and was more or less himself by sundown in the summer and late spring. In fall and winter the sun set too early and usually caught him frowning at his own hands or staring out the window until the window reflected Tatro and he was staring into his own eyes. Sometimes he didn't recognize himself. People saw him start and pull away from his reflection. He didn't look much different from it, anyway, all hollow-eyed and bluish gray from lack of sleep and smoky air. He was skinny and wrecked, with a drift of gray hair, but he would live to be a hundred, probably, people said. That kind of old whiteman always did.

So he was there as if waiting when Fleur entered with her son, who sat down next to her, vacant-eyed, and popped a sweet mallow-pillow into his mouth. He let it dissolve while he stared off into what passed for air inside that bar. The boy stared through drifts and curls of smoke. He stared through people who came and went. He stared but didn't see. The last thing people would have thought he noticed was the game played to either side and spread out before

191

him, but in fact, when he moved his lips and kept his eyes turned toward the ceiling as if reciting a fool's prayer, he was working out the whole game in his head from the first card played and he was gathering tics and habits, little sighs or intakes of breath. And he was learning the language of the toothpick. For instance, on which side Tatro chewed it when his hand was good. Jewett Tatro had a tender tooth on one side and if he had a bad hand Tatro would shift the toothpick in his jaw and bite down to distract himself. That toothpick told everything and the boy, the idiot, marked it and learned its habits while his mother played a demure game right next to him.

Yes, demure. She played modest and even and I don't need to tell you, dangerous. She played a snake's game. And of course she came back every night at the same time. She took no drink, but the marks of it were on her anyway. I could tell what she had done and, I hoped, quit doing down there in the city. There was still the reek of it and even the beginnings of ruin on her beautiful face. It hurt me to see this. It hurt us all, especially Margaret, who I noticed had gone unusually silent and thoughtful when it came to Fleur. Anyway, it did relieve me that Fleur didn't drink when she played, first that she still could—not drink, I mean. She wasn't that far gone. And I was also pleased because it indicated that she was going to pursue some strategy, the end of which I thought I knew already—everyone did, except Tatro. We all thought we knew why she was there.

Tatro knew the land had once been hers but didn't figure that she needed it back—not her in that white suit and that fancy car, which he coveted. Tatro got into the game every few days or so, which was another way that so much of our wealth ended up hung from nails above the bar. He liked to play for things because that made the game more interesting and also, even at that time, Tatro believed that the ways of making these old things were dying out and he was intrigued to have the last of such objects in his collection. So he played Fleur, having some vague idea of her reputation as a card player, and that she wasn't winning big from him and even occasionally losing a hand puffed him up. So far so transparent to me, to us all. But what about the boy beside her? What was he doing there?

It wasn't clear to me until some days had passed and Tatro was clearly bored of the game. A person's boredom always worked to Fleur's advantage. I sat in the corner of the bar, never touching a drop as I nursed too recent a memory of my shame. I sat there and drank orange soda fizz from a bottle. And I watched, night after night, for something to change. But what finally happened dismayed me. With no warning and in the middle of a game, Fleur called out, just after she'd lost a hand.

"Double whiskey!"

Down her cards went. Then the two shots.

"Oooh," she crowed, "that was good, that's better."

Then she ordered another.

"N'dawnis, gego minikweken!" I couldn't help advise her, but Fleur just turned to me with a look of indulgent amusement and kept on playing. She drank her poison more slowly, but then in short order it hit her and I saw her fumble. Her words thickened and her laugh, too loud, jarred the room. Her son sat next to her, impervious. Fleur saw things funny, funnier, and as she grew louder and more shrill everyone in the place collected around the table. When she shouted for more and in short order lost another hand to Tatro, more people slipped in through the door.

"I have no money now," she shrieked. "I am broke to the bone!"

She began to laugh and her caw of mirth was terrible to one who loved her. There is perhaps nothing quite socially painful as watching one you admire make herself foolish in other eyes. For yes, there were some now openly mocking her, saying how the Pillager used to be too good to look down at the shit on her shoes and now see what she's become. But others, most of the others, were very quiet. It was no small thing to see a woman who had represented something—oh yes, maybe fearful, maybe something that they didn't like—but represented the old ways, succumb to the new. We could feel that Pillager knowledge dissolving in the burning water. She was the last of the Pillagers, and to see her as a common drunk would take something out of every one of us. A terrible, thin, coldness slipped down my veins. Despair, though I couldn't name it right then, is a thin and bitter chill. I pulled my thin old shirt tight around my neck. I could not watch Fleur go lost.

"N'dawnis," I called out again from my place. "Come home with me, I'm begging you, now."

But I might as well have been talking to the bottle itself. She laid down her cards.

"Wait!" she told the others in a hissing, slurred undertone. "Let me go deal with the gabby old man."

Fleur reeled over to me and then stumbled into my lap. She gave a bray for a laugh, and dipped her head and spoke close to my ear. "Stay and watch what I have learned from you, old friend."

Her voice was sober as a rock. I sat back to enjoy myself.

The first thing that happened was Fleur lost another hand. Now she owed. That was the quicksand of Tatro's eternal game.

"I better fold and go home," she blurted.

"You can't," said Tatro.

"I got no money."

"Bet something else."

"I got nothing but my car."

"Bet that."

Fleur studied that idea, squinting an eye at him across the table as though his features were going blurry. The toothpick in Tatro's mouth jigged up and down. As soon as the car was mentioned, more people flooded in. Now the place was so crowded I had to creak up and stand on my chair to see the table. Fleur's fingers began to tap a little, as if she was nervous, and then she cried out.

"I need a whiskey on the house to clear my head!"

"Double, on the house," Tatro agreed. "Are you in with the Pierce-Arrow?" His toothpick now was tight-clenched. A light of panting greed was in his eye. The white of hubcaps. The chrome strip. The purring beauty of its expensive motor. From the beginning, from her first drink, he'd started to feel in his hands the steering wheel. Now his foot was pressing on the gas.

"What do you bet in return? What you got besides this place? I don't want this place!" She laughed at her own wit. She was the only one though and there was now a gasp of breath around her as she slipped from her chair and fell onto the floor. She pulled herself up by gripping the table's edge. "Oh, I'm a little shkwebii," she sang in a dreamy slur. "What do you bet me?"

"She can't play," said a Kashpaw. "It's taking advantage."

"She got in the game she stays in the game," said Tatro. Those were the rules. A player played a hand as long as fingers could hold cards. And as others had at times invoked this rule and profited by it, no one could really by rights make an issue. But the question remained what Tatro would put up. He pointed to the wall.

"Take your pick."

"Nothing's worth my car."

"Then take all of it!"

"What else you got?"

Fleur asked and then she fell off her chair again, only when she did so this time she appeared to realize suddenly that she was too drunk to go on. "I ain't steady enough," she informed everyone around her. Then she made a move that clenched a triumph in Tatro's mind.

"I'm gonna give my hand over to n'gozis."

A perfectly legal move by the game's long hammered-out rules. If a player couldn't see the cards or had the wit to know his moves were stupid, it was acceptable to hand the cards to a relative. This was, in fact, the way the game sucked in more people. It had worked to Tatro's long-term advantage, and he thought it was working short term now. He looked at the boy.

"Change chairs with me an' play my han'," Fleur said to her son. A hushed groan pushed out of people when the boy's gaze wandered up. His round eyes were empty of all light of understanding, his face as blank as one of Father Damien's china dinner plates. Wordless, he moved to his mother's chair. Fleur took the stool beside him, holding herself upright by clutching his shoulder. She crooned dizzily.

"What you got, Tatro?"

Seeing a sure win now, Tatro smiled his gray smile.

"I have some land," he said in a precise voice. "One hundred sixty acres on the lake. They're worthless. No timber."

"Throw in the island too!" I croaked from my perch on the chair.

"Yes, the island," the others in the room took up my suggestion. A surge of anger went through them, for the hopelessness of memory bit into them each in a different way.

Tatro looked over at the boy again. Engrossed in a point in space just over Tatro's head, he seemed in an idiot's trance. His hands were folded in his lap. Now he brought one up and licked his palm and tried to touch the colorless swatches of his hair down. This childish gesture of embarrassment decided Tatro.

"All right, the land and the island for the car."

"Get the deeds! Get the papers to both!" Others took up my insistence and the papers were soon fetched, the car's from the glove box and the deed to the land from the black safe in the floor beneath the cash register. Now the papers sat on the table. Tatro and the boy cut for the deal. The boy got the deal and it was then that the life of him showed, Fleur's part of him, the Pillager. His gaze raked lower so it rested with dead calm on Tatro's face, but his hands! The boy's hands swooped out from his sleeves like starved birds and the cards flew and gathered and divided themselves with a grace that made Tatro gasp.

I don't know if it was then Tatro knew how thoroughly he had been taken, or when he realized that the foolish mask the boy wore was in fact both his real face and unreadable. But for sure he must have known it by the fourth hand and then the fifth. The bet was six hands out of ten and the boy took every one.

SIXTEEN

The Healing

Margaret

*A*FTER THE card game between
the boy and the Indian agent was finished, after Tatro had staggered off gasping, after everyone had melted from the celebration
that spilled out the bar onto the road and then followed my old
man home, we slept, exhausted, and rose the next day. We sat
together talking around the fire drinking morning tea and replay-
ing the game, the foolish and foolhardiness of Tatro, the bitter
twist of his luck, the surprised malice in his face. I could feel
Lulu just beyond the firelight. I knew she'd vanish if I spoke, so
I brought a plate into the bush and set it on the ground. My husband smoked an endless pipe and speculated.

"He will try to deny it, but there were too many witnesses. He will have to honor his signed agreement and transfer the land."

"My land is no good anyway," Fleur gloated, "according to him. Ishkonigan, the leftovers!" The pleasure in her voice was wild. Her movements were jerky, her face stark with exhaustion. She looked older and almost sick, yellow showed under the smooth sheen of her skin.

"You got what you came back for," I said, reading her looks and knowing that she'd been drinking, long and hard, off in the Cities, and now here. "The agent is shrewd and heartless. You bested him and should be glad."

"Geget. Mii nange." Fleur emphatically agreed, but her eyes, as they rested on the spoiled child who sat mute as a stump at the edge of the yard, were anxious with sorrow.

"My son," she called out. She never called him anything else but n'gozis. Addressed him as her son and never used his name—Christian or Ojibwe. As far as we were concerned, the boy was nameless. For sure, such a thing was no accident. I opened my mouth to ask Fleur to tell me his name, but then a thought stopped me, an answer. *She had not named him.* I knew this as sure as I knew my own name. Oh, he'd have a name for the records, for papers, surely. A name for chimookomaan law. He'd have a name for the whites to call him, but no name for his spirit.

"You haven't named your own son," I hissed at Fleur, outraged at her carelessness. "He's strange in the head because the spirits don't know him!"

"He's not strange in the head," Fleur said, but only half indignantly. She knew the truth. "How was I supposed to name him in that city? Who would dream a name for him? Who would smoke the pipe? Who would introduce his spirit to the name and help his spirit to embrace that name?"

"You," I said. But she looked down at the ground.

"I tried, n'gah," she said, calling me her mother, which hit me. Her voice was filled with tones of pain. "Nothing went right."

"There's more to it than that," I said, and then I knew. I knew it all as I looked at her staring at the ground, she in her pristine white outfit, she of the old will, she with my childhood friend Anaquot's bold eyes and Four Souls's grin. I knew everything about who she came from and yet who Fleur was eluded me as much as it eluded all who felt the air stir and the leaves speak in her presence, those who could not look at her directly and yet could not look away from her. I had not known until that moment. But I know shame when I see it.

"Go away from here," I said to my old man, "peel the fancy suit off that boy and take him out in your boat to fish."

"It's too early," said Nanapush.

"Dunk your head in the cold water and go," I insisted.

"No!" cried the boy, his teeth streaked brown. He stuck his red tongue out at me.

I leaned down, grabbed him by the ear, and spoke.

"I'll gut you like a fish and throw your head to the dogs if you don't obey me! Now get into the house. Change your clothes. There's an old pants and shirt on the hook by the door."

The boy was so surprised that he did as I told him, and Nanapush soon had the boat ready. They pulled away from shore, struck off onto the lake. When they were gone, I turned to Fleur. She sat on the stump by the door in her white suit, looking at the ground, her face almost as vacant of spirit and slack as her son's.

"I can smell the liquor on you, n'dawnis," I said. "You stay here. Don't go anywhere."

And so she sat quiet in the yard and let the sun beat down, let herself sweat and ruin the starch in the white cloth. The fabric wilted until it clung to her skin. I built up the fire underneath my big kettle. I went down to the lake ten times and filled a flour sack with water and hauled it to the kettle and dumped it in. I put fronds of white cedar into the water. I brought out my big tin bathing tub and set it up near the fire, filled it partly with more water from the lake. More cedar. When the tub was steaming full and fragrant, I went to Fleur. I raised her up.

"First the white-lady shoes and stockings," I said. She nodded, neatly rolled the stockings down her legs, balled them up, and put them in the tips of her shoes.

"Next, the skirt." That, she lowered to the ground. I picked it up and carefully folded it, set the skirt beside the shoes. Her slip was transparent panels with a hem of delicate lace. She took that off too, and the cleverly sewn satin-lined jacket, the blouse underneath, then everything. Fleur Pillager stood naked by the washtub, her hair down her back again but not so long as it was before, her slim legs reflecting the play of the sun in the cedar water.

Slowly, she lowered herself into the water. She sat in the tub and put both hands over her face. I used my copper dipper to pour the water over her. It fell in shining strings and rivers and streams. I wet her hair and soaped it, then rinsed every trace of soap from her hair and did the whole thing again. At last, I gave Fleur the final rinse with fresh hot water that I poured on her from a gourd dipper. I cleaned her face with a rag, washed her carefully, dabbing the cloth with great care around the beautiful shape of her eyes. I traced the curve of her ears, ran the rag down her neck then back up under her chin. I took her hand in mine, and then I washed up and down each arm. I washed each finger and polished each clear oval nail. Then I had her kneel in the tub as I scrubbed her lean back.

By then, Fleur Pillager was trying to hold herself back; but failing, she wept like a girl. Racking sobs built and died in her, violent and unashamed. "You should cry," I said, "you deserve to cry." I left her outside in the yard, let her finish washing herself with her own tears. I went into our cabin and I pulled the most precious thing I'd ever made from its hiding place under blankets, against the wall. I took my medicine dress from the box I had made for it out of birch bark.

I smoothed out the soft leather folds of the skirt, then lighted a braid of sweet grass, cleaned the dress off with the smoke. I brought the sweet grass to Fleur as she stood naked, drying off in the sun. The sun cast its warmth and leafy shadows across her back. The new young trees whispered and the waves slapped at the stone shore. I fanned the sweet grass smoke across her body with the wing of an eagle. I combed out her hair and fanned it also with the holy fragrance. As I purified Fleur, I sang to her. The song of return, the song of Four Souls, the song of her name. I sang an old lullaby that made her cry again as she'd last heard it from her long dead mother, Ogimaakwe, Anaquot, Four Souls—she was called all of those names. I sang the song belonging to the lake, which was taught to us in dreams by the lake itself, and I sang her mother's song.

"You put the heart of an owl under your tongue," I said. "You braved all the old wisdom. You scorned us. You did not listen. And yet we love you, n'dawnis. We have loved you all through this. Myself, old Margaret, who has the vanity to call herself Rushes Bear, loves you as does the crazy old man. Nanapush. Your mother's spirit and her grandmother's, all the way back through the generations, love you. Your father and his fathers, too. All of these spirits love you, and the spirits in the four layers of the earth and the four skies that exist above us. The crawlers, the fliers, the runners, the swimmers. You are loved in creation though you tried to destroy yourself."

She held up her arms and I lowered my medicine dress upon her, helped her shrug into it, told her about the vision I had to make it and how I had followed that vision down to each detail. Then I explained to her what she must do.

"You can't just drive back onto your home ground with a trunk of old bones," I told her. "Yes, I know what you carried home in that whiteman's car. Nor can you stab the earth with the high heels on your shoes or breathe your whiskey breath into home air. You know where the rock is by Matchimanito. That is the place where your mother's people have suffered and cried out and fasted and begged for mercy from the spirits. You know your power and the earth in your Pillager blood is the result of generations of hard sacrifice behind you. The strength of your ancestors should not find an ending in your weakness."

"Geget," she said. "Mii nange. I know it."

Her head hung to her chest and she looked tired, so tired. The racks of her graceful shoulders sagged hard. I felt a wash of pity for her. But there wasn't enough human pity in the world to help Fleur Pillager. She needed more, from another source. She needed help from her neglected spirits, and would find it only by fasting on the dark rock eight days and eight nights with all of her memories and her ghosts. "You must suffer with your relatives," I told her. "The living and the dead.

"I am putting you out on a rock on the side of the lake," I went on, "with nothing to help you but my medicine dress. My daughter, the sun will bake and burn you and destroy your ability to see, but this dress will save your vision so that you'll be forced to look within. It will get worse. Stinging flies will torture your skin and the zagimeg will suck your blood. This dress will allow them to bite right through. Then it will heal your wounds so that you'll be fresh for the insects each morning. Those tiny spirits will drive you past your limit. At night the wind will rake you, cold off the lake. The cold air will clench around your heart and you will be devoured by the cold, but this dress will not let you die. No food will pass your lips for the eight days you will lie on this rock, but this medicine dress will not let you starve to death, nor will it feed you or give you water. Every night after the fourth day I will come to you with just enough water to keep life in your body. This dress will intensify your hunger and allow you the privilege to suffer. This dress will listen to you, Four Souls, crying out for kindness and mercy in spite of your terrible will.

"Again, you will remember every dear one you lost, those you have forced yourself to forget in order to survive. You threw your souls out. You lived. Now you must weep over those who died in your place. Mourn your dead properly so you can live properly, Fleur. Weep yourself sick. And then from your heart, from under your skin, and from the arrogant shell you call the surface of your mind will come the pain of understanding your loneliness. This dress will force you to enter the darkness of your spirit. Your empty spirit. Your angry, lost, devouring, last soul. You will be left there, alone, and you will not know why you are alone. For you are a beggar in this life, Fleur Pillager. Four Souls. All the power you were given and all the luck that drove you to the Cities, all the cruelty that lay in your heart toward those who wronged you, all the devotion to the land and to your stubborn idea comes to nothing before one truth—your first child does not love you and your second child doesn't know how. How can they love a woman who has wasted her souls? How can they love a mother who forgot to guard their tenderness, and her own? How can they love a woman who can suffer anything and do anything? Forget your power and your strength. Let the dress kill you. Let the dress save you. Let yourself break down and need your boy and your girl."

Your name was Four Souls, I said, and my voice was neither gentle or kind, but neutral in its observation, cold as I listed Fleur's names. Four Souls, but you haven't got four souls anymore. Your name was Fleur because the French trader's wife favored you. It is not Fleur. No more is it Fleur. No matter what people call you. Your name was Leaves Her Daughter. White Woman. Zhooniyaa. Your name was All Wrong. All Too Different. Impossible. Your name was Sorrow like the dog your aunt slaughtered so her child should eat. Your name was Kills Him Once. Kills Him Again. Kills Him Over and Over. I'm not faulting you for your revenge, but what did it get you? Are you satisfied when you look into the blank eyes of your son and when your daughter turns aside from you in the road? When she won't call you Mother? When she spits on the ground to hear your name?

You are loved to extremes, and you are hated to extremes, Fleur Pillager. Now is the time for you to walk the middle way.

If you make it through the next eight days, I will give you my medicine dress. Not only that, I will give you the name that goes with it. For the dress has its own name, which it told to me while I was making it. When you are finally brave enough to experience fear, you will ask the dress for its name and plead for it to help you. If you ask humbly enough, the dress will tell you, and if you have the strength to accept that name, then the dress will give its name to your spirit. You and I and the dress will know who you are. Maybe we'll tell my no-good husband Nanapush, too. Your name will live inside of you. Your name will help you heal. Your name will tell you how long to live and when to give up life. When the time comes for you to die, you will be called by that name and you will answer. For you have been lonely so long, you nameless one, you spirit, and it will comfort you to finally be recognized here upon this earth.

End of the Story

Nanapush

*T*HE BIRDS are gone, and with them, on their wings, the thunder and the lightning. The skin of ice grows farther out onto the lake and the wind turns the raindrops to dust. The dogs born on the reservation look like Shesheeb's famous mutt now—all round-headed runts. I take credit for their ugliness. I am at peace. My tracks drag. This is old age, at last. My eyes are weary. My heart is full. My favorite parts of me limp and undemanding. Finally, I can see the shape of all that's happened and all that is to come. Within me there has always burned an urge to see how things turn out. To know the story.

Now that I know the story, I can rest.

The woman once called Fleur Pillager, and now named Four Souls as well as another name nobody speaks, is now understood by the spirits. Like the spirits, she lives quiet in the woods. No road leads to her place. Hardly even a path. She doesn't drown men anymore or steal their tongues, she doesn't gamble. She doesn't rub her hands with powders of human bones. She doesn't sing, at least we can't hear her above the rustle of dollar bills flying from our hands to the government and papers and more legal forms flapping down to cover us in return. Change is chaos and pain. There was no order in our making. This reservation came about in a time of desperation and upon it we will see things occur more desperate yet. When I look at the scope and the drift of our history, I see that we have come out of it with something, at least. This scrap of earth. This ishkonigan. This leftover. We've got this and as long as we can hold on to it we will be some sort of people.

Once we were a people who left no tracks. Now we are different. We print ourselves deeply on the earth. We build roads. The ruts and skids of our wheels bite deep and the bush recedes. We make foundations for our buildings and sink wells beside our houses. Our shoes are hard and where we go it is easy to follow. I have left my own tracks, too. I have left behind these words. But even as I write them down I know they are merely footsteps in snow. They will be gone by spring. New growth will cover them, and me. That green in turn will blacken, snow will obscure us all, but, my sons and daughters, sorrow is a useless thing. Much as the grass dies, the wind exhausts its strength, the tree topples in a light breeze, the dead buffalo melt away into the prairie ground or are plowed into newly scratched-out fields, all things familiar dissolve into strangeness. Even our bones nourish change, and even a people who lived so close to the bone and were saved for thousands of generations by a practical philosophy, even such people as we, the Anishinaabeg, can sometimes die, or change, or change and become.